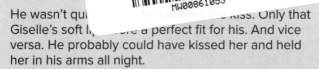

Before he k

He wasn't qui... ...kiss. Only that Giselle's soft li... ...e a perfect fit for his. And vice versa. He probably could have kissed her and held her in his arms all night.

But before they went much further, Quincy did the honorable thing in wanting to make sure this was really what she wanted and neither would have any regrets—so he pulled back.

Giselle seemed to be of the same mind as she touched her swollen lips and told him, "Thank you, Quincy, for...a very pleasant evening."

He nodded, gazing at her eyes intently. "Thanks for inviting me."

By the time he left, Quincy was already looking forward to spending more time with Giselle. And all that came with the desirous territory.

In memory of my cherished mother, Marjah Aljean, a devoted lifelong fan of Harlequin romance and romantic suspense novels, who inspired me to excel in my personal and professional lives. To H. Loraine, the true love of my life and very best friend, whose support has been unwavering through the many terrific years together, as well as the many loyal fans of my romance, suspense, mystery and thriller fiction published over the years. Lastly, a nod goes out to my great Harlequin editors, Denise Zaza and Emma Cole, for the wonderful opportunity to lend my literary voice and creative spirit to the Harlequin Intrigue line, as well as Miranda Indrigo, the wonderful concierge, who serendipitously led me to success with Harlequin Intrigue.

HIDING IN ALASKA

R. BARRI FLOWERS

Harlequin
INTRIGUE

Harlequin®
INTRIGUE™

Recycling programs for this product may not exist in your area.

ISBN-13: 978-1-335-45730-1

Hiding in Alaska

Copyright © 2025 by R. Barri Flowers

 Harlequin Enterprises ULC
22 Adelaide St. West, 41st Floor
Toronto, Ontario M5H 4E3, Canada
www.Harlequin.com

Printed in U.S.A.

R. Barri Flowers is an award-winning author of crime, thriller, mystery and romance fiction featuring three-dimensional protagonists, riveting plots, unexpected twists and turns, and heart-pounding climaxes. With an expertise in true crime, serial killers and characterizing dangerous offenders, he is perfectly suited for the Harlequin Intrigue line. Chemistry and conflict between the hero and heroine, attention to detail and incorporating the very latest advances in criminal investigations are the cornerstones of his romantic suspense fiction. Discover more on popular social networks and Wikipedia.

Books by R. Barri Flowers

Harlequin Intrigue

Bureaus of Investigation Mysteries

Killer in Shellview County
Hiding in Alaska

The Lynleys of Law Enforcement

Special Agent Witness
Christmas Lights Killer
Murder in the Blue Ridge Mountains
Cold Murder in Kolton Lake
Campus Killer
Mississippi Manhunt

Hawaii CI

The Big Island Killer
Captured on Kauai
Honolulu Cold Homicide

Visit the Author Profile page at Harlequin.com.

CAST OF CHARACTERS

Giselle Kinard—A dance instructor who flees an obsessed ex-fiancé in Chesapeake, Virginia, for a small town in Alaska, Taller's Creek. She now fears he may have found her when people in her orbit start to die, as he'd promised were she to ever leave.

Quincy Lankard—An Alaskan Native investigator for the Alaska Bureau of Investigation who looks into a series of suspicious deaths that may be connected to Giselle, the attractive bookshop worker whom he is falling for in spite of his feeling that she is holding back on something important to his case.

Daniel Malaterre—A special agent in charge with the Federal Bureau of Investigation who goes the extra mile in providing critical information to assist Quincy in going after a stalker and possible killer who may be targeting Giselle.

Miriam Fontaine—A police sergeant who investigates some untimely deaths, leaving her to believe that there may be more to them than meets the eye.

Jacinta Cruz—A documentary producer who believes she may have found the man of her dreams, but she could be making the mistake of her life.

Justin Buckner—A fixated and manipulative financial planner who wants to make his ex-fiancée pay dearly for running away from their relationship. But not before he targets other women she knows in making good on his warnings to that effect.

Prologue

Giselle Kinard had always assumed she was smart enough to choose the right person to be in a solid relationship with. Boy, had she been wrong. How could she have been so blind? Justin Buckner was anything but the right man to build a future with. Much less become her fiancé.

At the age of twenty-eight, she was still dealing with the recent deaths of her parents, both succumbing to illnesses one soon after the other. Feeling vulnerable, Giselle had thought she was ready to move on when she'd met Justin at her studio in Chesapeake, Virginia, where she was a dance instructor. She had been interested in dancing from a very young age, when her mother had made her take ballet lessons. This would ultimately lead to her receiving a bachelor of arts degree from the dance program at Old Dominion University in Norfolk, Virginia.

Two years older, Justin Buckner was very good looking, tall, golden haired, blue eyed and in great shape. He'd been charming, sure of himself, a successful financial planner and very easy to teach how to ballroom dance. Not to mention he'd been as single and available as she'd been and eager to get involved with the right woman.

Was it any wonder that she'd been swept off her feet by him? They had only been dating for six months when Justin had asked Giselle to marry him, declaring his strong love for her. Though she'd hesitated to say yes, sensing something was off with him, she'd ultimately gone against her instincts and put her trust in the man, and agreed to marry him.

But the more time they'd spent together—mainly in his huge waterfront estate with magnificent views of the Elizabeth River—the more Giselle had begun to pull away from him before they could walk down the aisle. As she'd lost sight of who she was under his thumb, she'd seen the dark side of Justin. He'd become possessive, domineering, controlling, jealous, irrational and, frankly, dangerous. She'd hated it when he'd warned her more than once, "Don't test me, Giselle!"

She viewed that as much more than just a veiled threat. Especially when he'd outright cautioned her that were she to ever leave him, he would go after everyone Giselle knew, one by one, saving her for last but certainly not least.

She believed he meant business and would sooner see her dead than allow her to walk away from the life he felt was meant to be for them as husband and wife.

But even that intimidation was not enough for Giselle to go through with a doomed marriage that she knew would be very wrong. At least for her.

Leaving Justin and getting a restraining order to keep him at a safe distance was not an option. At least not a viable one. How many times had she read about a woman being murdered by her current or former partner after he'd blatantly disregarded a protection order and come after her?

Giselle was determined not to end up another statistic of a domestic-related homicide while Justin possibly ended up using his family's money and influence to beat the rap. Then another woman or more potential victims could wind up in his crosshairs down the line.

That was when she made the decision to run. Some place where he would never find her. With the lease to her apartment up, the few things she had already placed in storage and plans to ditch her red Toyota Camry, she was set to make her escape. Having stashed away some money, including a small inheritance from her parents, she could afford to leave everything behind, painful as it was, and start over.

Giselle could only hope that by putting time and distance between them, Justin would get past her ending their engagement—including leaving the diamond engagement ring he'd given her and a key to his house on the granite countertop in the gourmet kitchen while he was out—and stop looking for her.

Maybe then she would be able to return home and reclaim her life.

Or was that too much to hope for, given the vindictiveness Giselle knew was intrinsic in his nature, were they to ever lay eyes on one another again?

She didn't take time to have any second thoughts before going into hiding.

JUSTIN BUCKNER WAS incensed when he came home from work and spotted the engagement ring and house key on the kitchen counter. It told him everything he needed to know but didn't want to believe.

Giselle had left him. Left their relationship before it ever became official in two months.

Did she really think it would be so simple to walk away from what they had?

He had sold his parents on Giselle. Even when they'd believed she wasn't good enough for him, he'd believed otherwise. They were perfect together. She would be a great mother to their children. No matter that she needed his guidance when Giselle managed to step outside the line that he'd set from time to time, only for him to steer her right back on track as he wanted.

He wasn't about to let her slip from his grasp and take up with someone else. Not in this lifetime.

Defeat wasn't in his DNA. At least when it came to his choice for a lifelong partner.

Giselle was that woman. He'd known it the moment he'd laid his blue eyes upon her, smitten with Giselle's dark-haired, green-eyed beauty, with a slender body to match.

She was his and only his. Sooner than later, she would realize that.

But only after he taught her a costly lesson so that she would get the message loud and clear. Once and for all.

Getting on his cell phone, Justin called Giselle, only to get her voice mail. He demanded that she pick up but was ignored. His nostrils flared at this sign of disobedience.

He checked the GPS tracker he'd installed on her phone and saw that she was at her apartment.

Storming across the walnut hardwood flooring in his

great room, Justin disregarded the custom-made furnishings and was out the door.

Moments later, he was driving away from his property in a blue BMW 430i coupe. He tried Giselle again on his cell, but she wouldn't answer him. Why would she put him in a position of having to punish her for this brazen act of disloyalty?

Did she really think that by simply ditching her ring it would be over between them?

Not hardly.

Think and think again.

No one left him. And lived to talk about it.

Unbeknownst to Giselle, this had happened once before. His last girlfriend, Jenna Sweeney, had made the foolish mistake of trying to end their relationship.

He'd made sure she'd paid the price with her life.

Unless he could get Giselle to come back on her own and promise to never pull a stunt like this again, she would suffer the same fate.

It took him a few minutes to get to her apartment complex on Ferris Drive. Had it been up to him, she would have moved into his place by now—he'd given her a key to show how serious he was about this. But she'd refused to do so till after they were married.

He had gone along with this, though now he wondered if he should have applied more pressure to get married instead of waiting.

When he got out of the car, Justin never bothered to look for Giselle's vehicle in the parking lot, figuring it was out of his view. Instead he headed straight for her second-story apartment. Using his own key that she had given him, he opened the door and went inside.

To his surprise, he saw that the place was empty. He checked his cell phone GPS tracker. It indicated that her device was at that location. He called it and realized that the phone was in a trash can in the small kitchen.

"That bitch," Justin muttered angrily, hating himself for underestimating Giselle. *Run, but you can't hide forever*, he thought.

He would find her—if it was the last thing he ever did. And she would never know what had hit her.

Until it was too late.

Chapter One

Taller's Creek, Alaska.

The quaint town of less than five thousand inhabitants, located in the Kenai Peninsula Borough, was about as far away from Chesapeake, Virginia, as could be.

That was certainly how Giselle Kinard had seen it as she had settled in there comfortably at the age of thirty-one, believing she had successfully evaded her ex-fiancé, Justin Buckner. He had refused to take no for an answer when she'd wanted to end their relationship and any plans for marrying him, once his true colors had come out in plain and frightening view.

It had been nearly three years since her brazen escape. First she'd bounced around a few states in the Lower 48—going to Atlanta, Georgia; then Huntsville, Alabama; then San Antonio, Texas and Oakland, California. But she'd felt she was constantly looking over her shoulder, sure Justin would track her down, working odd jobs to survive before making her way to Alaska eighteen months ago.

It seemed the perfect escape. Taller's Creek was tucked away in the Gulf Coast Region and offered her the refuge Giselle had sought. There were enough interesting things to see and do to keep her from getting bored, while staying safe at the same time.

She had moved into a cozy little one-bedroom apartment with lots of windows on a dead-end street in a wooded area by Teary Lake, furnished it with second-hand but attractive contemporary furniture, adopted a Burmese kitten and gotten a job at a bookstore as a sales associate. Though she'd loved her old job and had been good at it, she didn't dare continue to be a dance instructor while on the run, certain that this would be something Justin would be looking for in his quest to find her.

Over time she had made a few friends, who thankfully didn't ask too many questions. Taking no chances, she didn't use social media under her name, went out of her way to avoid being photographed by anyone and resisted contacting people from her past life for fear that it could put them in harm's way. Or lead Justin to locating and coming after her.

So far, so good, Giselle told herself as she got ready for work on this mid-July Saturday morning, slipping into a purple button-up chiffon shirt, jeans and flats. She had dyed her long hair blond and cut it into a shoulder-length shag style with curtain bangs.

Maybe her ex-fiancé had more pressing issues to deal with than discovering her whereabouts and making good on his threats, she considered, moving across the hardwood flooring while glancing at the mostly closed vinyl shutters on the windows. About a year or so ago, she had used a computer at the library to look him up and had been surprised—or maybe not so much—to see that Justin was under federal investigation for bilking many of his clients out of amounts that went into the hundreds of thousands of dollars.

But checking on this periodically, Giselle was disappointed to see that the investigation seemed to have stalled, in spite of the indication that it was still ongoing. She wondered if Justin might be able to somehow worm his way out of going to prison. If so, it would mean that he would continue to pose a danger to her.

At least in theory.

Or was it more than that?

Though she had nothing more than a feeling at this point, something deep within Giselle sensed that she still wasn't entirely out of the woods yet where it concerned Justin.

Or had she allowed him to get into her head way too much, with no contact since the day she'd walked away from the nightmarish life she'd had—and would have had beyond that—with him?

She fed her rambunctious kitten, Muffin, who had been abandoned before Giselle had come to her rescue, then she grabbed her crossbody bag and headed out the door.

Moments later, she was behind the wheel of her silver Honda CR-V and on the road. Giselle took in the sights and sounds of Taller's Creek, amazed by its geographically diverse surroundings that included great beaches, kettle lakes, mountains and wetlands.

A stone's throw from Soldotna, Taller's Creek, alongside Owen Bay, sat on the western side of the Kenai National Wildlife Refuge, a nearly two-million-acre wildlife habitat preserve with an abundance of wildlife, such as black and brown bears, caribou, Dall sheep, eagles, mountain goats, moose, trumpeter swans and wolves.

She'd taken up birdwatching as a hobby, with various land birds, shorebirds, seabirds and waterfowl getting her attention. Beyond that, as an active person, she loved to hike, jog, cross-country ski and river float whenever she could.

Honestly, Giselle wasn't sure if she would ever be ready to give this up. Though she occasionally grew homesick and missed being a dance instructor (but didn't dare make it easier to be found), with her parents gone and no friends Justin had allowed her to get close to, Giselle felt she was in a good place right now.

Until proven otherwise.

She reached the Taller's Creek Books building on Milton Lane, parked in the back and went inside. The independent bookstore was practically a landmark, having been around for half a century, and had gone through several owners. The current owner, Jill Kekiwi, a sixty-five-year-old widow, had bought the place twelve years ago to keep her busy after retiring from her school-teacher job when her husband had died. She had hired Giselle on the spot, sensing her need for employment and believing her to be a good fit for the midsized bookseller that had two other full-time sales associates, Wesley Abbott and Ellen Ebsen, and one part-timer, a college student named Sadie Pisano.

"Morning," Jill greeted her cheerfully as Giselle walked up to her.

"Good morning." She flashed her teeth at the medium-sized woman with white hair in a chopped pixie style and brown eyes behind browline glasses.

"Don't get too relaxed. There's a customer waiting for you…"

"Really?" Giselle turned around and saw her friend, Neve Chenoweth, standing by the counter, holding a stack of books. "I'm on it," Giselle told her boss.

Jill smiled. "Good to know."

Giselle walked over to Neve, whose brown eyes were buried in one of the books, and got her attention. "Hey."

Neve, who was African American, Giselle's same age and five feet, seven inches tall, had short brown hair in a feathered cut with blond highlights. She looked up and said, "There you are."

"Here I am." Giselle grinned at the US Air Force veteran, who had chosen to remain in Alaska after being honorably discharged. "Sorry to keep you waiting, but aren't you supposed to be hiking this morning?"

"Yep," Neve admitted, dressed for the excursion. "But I wanted to drop by and pick up some books to deep dive into later."

"I see." Giselle took them from her and sat them on the counter before going to the other side to ring up the purchase. "Well, you've come to the right place—and thanks for allowing me to be your sales associate."

Neve laughed. "What are friends for, right?"

"Right." Giselle got her credit card. "Maybe next time we can go hiking together." As they had on other occasions when she had the time to be adventurous and work up a good sweat.

"Sure," Neve agreed. "Whenever you're ready, let me know."

Giselle put the books into a bag and was about to ask Neve if she was back on the market after dumping the last guy she had been seeing but decided not to go there. It would invariably result in being asked about her own love life, which to Giselle had admittedly been pretty much nonexistent since moving to Alaska. She had gone out with someone every now and then but mostly chose to keep to herself and not get too serious about anyone for fear of history repeating itself in being attached to a controlling, unstable and dangerous man. "Here you go," she said, handing her friend the bag.

"Thanks." Neve eyed her. "So, what are you doing tonight?"

"Not much," Giselle had to admit. "Probably catch up on some chores, watch television."

"I have a better idea," she said, smiling. "A few of us are meeting up at the Owl's Den. Why don't you come?"

As she had no good reason to reject the idea of hanging out with friends at a popular bar in town, Giselle agreed. "Count me in."

"Cool." Neve licked her lips. "I'll call you later."

"I'll call you first," she countered.

"Okay."

Neve walked away, and Giselle watched for a moment as she walked out the door. She barely noticed the tall man wearing a hoodie and loose clothing who followed Neve from the store. Other than the fact that it didn't appear as though he had purchased any books.

Giselle didn't give it much thought as another customer came up to the counter.

QUINCY LANKARD SAT in a swivel seat of a black leather office chair at his wooden workstation as an investigator assigned to the regional major crimes unit of the Alaska

Bureau of Investigation on Kalifornsky Beach Road in Soldotna, Alaska. A branch of the Alaska Department of Public Safety's Alaska State Troopers, the ABI had been his employer ever since he'd gotten his bachelor's degree in criminal justice from the University of Alaska Fairbanks ten years ago.

An Alaskan Native and member of the Eyak, he was honored to represent Indigenous peoples of the state in law enforcement, wanting to make sure that justice was served equally to anyone who violated the law. At thirty-two, a few months removed from turning thirty-three, he was still single and childless, much to the chagrin of his parents and younger and married sister, Olivia, who had two great kids.

Though he, too, hoped to someday find that right person to walk down the aisle with and become the mother of his children, Quincy was not desperate enough to rush into something he'd only end up regretting. Everything in life would come at the right time, he firmly believed. That included marrying the woman of his dreams and going from there.

He turned his focus to his latest investigation. A home invasion in Soldotna had turned deadly, with the fifty-three-year-old homeowner, Abigail Tavares, the victim. The ABI, in conjunction with the Anchorage Police Department, had tracked down the home invader in Anchorage, Alaska, one hundred and twenty miles away. Matthew Fife, a twenty-six-year-old with an extensive criminal history, had been charged with first-degree murder and burglary.

Quincy had personally slapped the cuffs onto the suspect and was glad to have him off the streets. While savoring that victory for a moment, a 911 call came in from the Soldotna Public Safety Communications Center, the dispatch center for the Kenai Peninsula Borough.

"We have a report of a dead female found near the Pippen Trail," the dispatcher said somberly.

"That's not good..." Quincy muttered musingly, his brown-gray eyes hardening. He immediately suspected that the deceased person was Neve Chenoweth, a thirty-one-year-old hiker who had been missing for two days now. An AST search and rescue team had been sent to the area in Taller's Creek after cell phone pings had indicated that the woman's phone was in the vicinity. So, was this her? And how had she died?

Not wanting to jump the gun, Quincy kept all options on the table. He noted that a year ago a male hiker had been found dead in the same area, and it had been ruled an accidental fall down a gulley. Though he suspected something similar might have happened here, Quincy was duty bound to investigate any death of an otherwise healthy individual as suspicious until proven otherwise.

After briefing the lieutenant who headed the command staff on the situation, Quincy rose from his desk, a solid six-feet, four-inch frame in full uniform. He was wearing a felt campaign hat above thick, trimmed dark hair, a ballistic vest and a body camera. A loaded Glock 22 40 S&W caliber handgun sat in his tactical thigh holster. He headed out, steeling himself for the grim discovery.

After climbing into his white Ford Police Interceptor Utility SUV, Quincy drove away from the regional MCU and headed northeast on Kenai Spur Highway toward Taller's Creek. He wondered what the last thoughts had been of the deceased hiker, assuming there had even been time to take stock of her life and where she'd wanted it to go. Maybe she could still get somewhere on the other side.

When he arrived on the scene at the Pippen Trail on Klatton Road, Quincy exited his vehicle and made his way past search personnel before meeting up with Search and Rescue Coordinator Gabe McAuliffe.

Nearly as tall as him but thinner, with blond hair in a high-and-tight cut, the fortysomething Gabe furrowed his brow and said sourly, "We've located Neve Chenoweth… Sorry it came to this."

"Me too," Quincy replied, having already anticipated such. "Where is she?"

"This way…"

He followed Gabe down a trail through a forested area and onto a side trail above Owen Bay, where Quincy spotted the body. It was invisible from the main trail and lying awkwardly. Neve Chenoweth was African American, tall and slender. Her short, feathered hair was reddened with blood, as her head lay atop a large rock.

Gabe uttered, "I'm guessing that she tripped accidentally while jogging, hit her head and was out like a light."

"Maybe," Quincy said thoughtfully. He could imagine some other scenarios. Such as someone hitting her from behind. Or perhaps she'd been suicidal and deliberately followed those dark impulses. "We'll see what the State Medical Examiner's Office has to say."

"Right," Gabe agreed. "Aside from that, there's the difficult task of family and friends having to come to terms with the reality that Neve is gone."

"Yeah, there is that." Quincy pinched his nose, knowing this was the hard part. Especially when, presumably, no one had seen this coming. Or had someone?

THREE HOURS LATER, Quincy entered Taller's Creek Books. As part of his investigation, pending the autopsy report, he wanted to reach out to Neve Chenoweth's friends in hopes of getting a complete picture of her last hours of life. Maybe give him a different perspective to lean on for the deceased, whom he'd discovered had been originally from Syracuse, New York, where much of her family lived, and had served in the US military.

He took note of the slender woman in her early thirties who was putting books on a shelf in the children's section. *That must be her*, he thought instinctively and headed her way.

"Hi," Quincy said, getting her attention. "Are you Giselle Kinard?"

"Yes," she spoke softly.

He could tell she was gorgeous without needing to look too hard. She gazed at him with the loveliest, though clearly saddened, green eyes he had ever seen. They were on a nice heart-shaped face, along with a dainty nose, full lips and a small cleft in her chin. Her shaggy blond hair rested on her shoulders, and he liked the bangs. She was wearing a ruffled short-sleeve rose-colored blouse, black straight-leg pants and brown loafers.

"I'm Trooper Quincy Lankard with the Alaska Bureau of Investigation," he told her. "We're looking into the death of Neve Chenoweth."

"You are…?" She batted her eyes, ill at ease.

"It's just routine," he tried to reassure her. "Though it appears her death was a tragic accident—which the autopsy should confirm—the ABI still has to sign off on that. As I understand it, you were one of Ms. Chenoweth's friends. And furthermore, the time line indicates that she purchased some books here shortly before she went hiking—"

On that note, Giselle's legs seemed to give out on her, prompting Quincy to gladly come to her rescue, holding her steady. He liked the way she felt in his arms—soft and supple—while wondering curiously if there was something in particular that could have triggered this reaction to his news.

Chapter Two

If she was being honest about it, Giselle had to admit that it felt surprisingly natural to be in the powerful arms of the good-looking trooper. Were the circumstances different, she could imagine it being something that she could get used to in a hurry. As it was, they were in the middle of a bookstore, and he had merely reflexively come to her aid before Giselle's legs gave out from beneath her and she went sprawling embarrassingly down to the floor.

Giselle wasn't quite sure why she reacted that way. Yes, she was still reeling at the news from a little earlier that her friend Neve Chenoweth had been found dead by the Pippen Trail. The speculation was that it was likely accidental. Trooper Quincy Lankard seemed to believe that would prove to be the case.

So why had she freaked out at that moment?

If you even think about ever leaving me, Giselle, just know that you'll pay for it in ways you can't even imagine. I'll go after everyone you care about...or cares about you, even a little...one by one. Saving you for last.

Her ex-fiancé Justin Buckner's chilling words replayed in Giselle's head. Could he have found her and made his threat come true?

"Are you all right?" Trooper Lankard asked in a deep voice, still holding her close to his rock-hard body as though never wanting to let her go.

"I'm fine," she stated, making herself believe this to be true as Giselle extricated herself from his arms and made sure her legs wouldn't buckle again.

"You sure about that?" He trained deep brown eyes shaded in gray at her with mild concern.

"Yes." She colored while quickly sizing him up. Aside from being very tall in comparison to her height of five-seven with his uniform seemingly showing off every muscle in his body, she guessed the handsome trooper to be in his early thirties, like her. He had a square face and strong jawline with a straight nose and round chin that was smooth shaven. Though he was wearing a blue campaign hat, she could see that he had rich black hair cut short in a military style and could imagine running her hands through it.

"I just had a moment," she tried to explain. "Losing a friend like that so suddenly has been difficult to process—"

"I understand," he said in a sympathetic tone of voice. "Why don't we sit and talk..." He angled his eyes toward a nearby set of velvet accent reading chairs.

Giselle nodded. "Okay."

She walked ahead of him, and they sat down at the same time before Trooper Lankard stretched his long legs out and asked gently, "So, how long have you known Ms. Chenoweth?"

"About a year and a half."

"Do you know if she ever suffered from PTSD?" He waited a beat, then said, "I understand that Ms. Chenoweth was a Tactical Air Control Party specialist with the US Air Force before her discharge."

"Neve never mentioned that she'd experienced PTSD," Giselle responded, while wondering why it would matter in any event if her death had truly been an accident. "But that doesn't mean she didn't choose to keep it to herself."

"True. I can dig deeper here with the military if it becomes necessary in the investigation, but that likely won't be the case," he stressed, then leaned back and scratched his chin thoughtfully. "Any indication that Ms. Chenoweth was suicidal…?"

"What?" Giselle's brow furrowed, surprised that he would even go there. "Are you suggesting that Neve killed herself?" she snapped.

"Nothing of the sort." His voice dropped an octave. "I have no reason to believe that we're looking at a suicide here, based on what we know thus far. Just trying to cover the bases as a prelude to closing the case. Sorry if you took umbrage to the question."

Maybe I was a bit over the top or too defensive, Giselle told herself regretfully. The trooper had every right to want to know what Neve's state of mind might have been before her death. Even if the notion that she would take her own life was absurd.

"It's okay." Giselle softened her voice. "I know you're just doing your job. In any event, the answer is no, Neve was in no way suicidal. She loved life too much to want to leave it the way that she did."

"Figured as much," he said coolly. "Anyone who likes to hike has to enjoy living and being in touch with nature."

"Yes, that pretty much describes the Neve I know—

knew," Giselle said, still trying to come to terms with thinking of her in the past tense.

"All right." Trooper Lankard flashed a crooked grin. "One more question and I'll get out of your hair, figuratively speaking." He paused. "Did she always go hiking alone? I'm only asking because even for experienced hikers, partnering up with someone is always a good idea—if only to be able to call for help should one or the other have a problem. That could have made the difference between life and death—"

Giselle agreed on the face of it, wishing she had accompanied her friend to the Pippen Trail. On the other hand, accidents did happen as part of life. Maybe there was nothing that could have made a difference in the outcome. Unless it was proven that Neve's death had been no accident after all.

"Neve often hiked alone," Giselle informed the trooper. "She liked exploring Alaska on her own. But she wasn't opposed to hiking with others, including me. If only that had been the case this time…" Giselle shuddered at the thought that Neve had had to die with no one around to offer comfort.

"You can't blame yourself," he said firmly. "I'm sure she wouldn't want you to. We all make choices that we can't always run away from and just have to deal with them, for better or worse…"

That comment struck a nerve with Giselle. She had made the choice to run away from the life she'd had in Virginia. And had to live with the consequences— mainly leaving everything behind and not being able to look back for her own safety. Fortunately, things had fallen into place for her up to this point. So long as she didn't count the fact that one of the first people who had befriended her upon arriving in Taller's Creek was now dead—reminding Giselle that bad things could still happen, even when you least expected it.

She realized that Trooper Lankard had stood up and moved closer to her. "I'd better let you get back to stocking children's books on the shelves," he spoke evenly. "Thanks for your time."

"No problem." Giselle quickly got to her feet, meeting his warm eyes. At the mention of children, she couldn't help but wonder if he had any. Somehow it seemed like the trooper would make a good father. At the very least, she could tell that he took his job seriously. Even if he had to deal with such tragedies as death. Impetuously she said to him, "In case you're interested, we're having a candlelight vigil at eight p.m. tonight at the Pippen Trail, to honor Neve's life."

"I'll be there," he said, as if not needing to give it a single thought.

"Okay." Giselle smiled at him, feeling like he truly cared about people. He was the type of person she could imagine, at least in theory, getting to know better outside of his official capacity. Or would that be unwise, after her nightmarish relationship with Justin? "See you then," she told the trooper simply, masking the eagerness to do just that.

"You will," he promised and tipped the brim of his hat courteously, then walked away.

No sooner had Quincy Lankard left the bookstore and Giselle was contemplative as she returned to stocking shelves when Wesley Abbott, one of the other sales associates, came over.

In his midforties and gangly, with brown hair in a spiked mohawk and blue eyes behind wire-rimmed glasses, Wesley stated curiously, "Saw you talking to the state trooper. What was that all about?"

"He's looking into the death of my friend, Neve Chenoweth," Giselle answered, holding a new children's book in her hands. By now, she was sure that everyone in Taller's Creek had heard about the tragedy, including Wesley, whom she hadn't spoken to since learning the news herself.

"Yeah, I'm sorry about that." He touched his glasses. "Do they still believe it was an accident?"

"As far as I'm aware," she replied, knowing that they were waiting for the autopsy report to make it official. "As an ABI investigator, Trooper Lankard is questioning people Neve knew as part of the routine in order to close the case."

"I see." Wesley was holding two hardcover copies of a just-released spy novel. "Well, if you ever need someone to talk to about what happened to your friend, I'm a good listener."

Giselle batted her lashes. Was he actually coming on to her? Or legitimately concerned about her peace of mind? Though she didn't know him all that well, in spite of working at the same bookstore for months now, last she'd heard he was in a committed relationship with the Norwegian woman he lived with. Had that changed?

Giselle smiled thinly. "I'll keep that in mind."

He nodded and walked away. She turned back to the shelf she was working on, knowing it was a good distraction. Even if it was hard to get what had happened to Neve out of her head. Perhaps the vigil would serve as a means to not only pay her respects but help her try to get on with her life, which had already seen more than its fair share of challenges to overcome.

THE CANDLELIGHT VIGIL was held at the Pippen Trail as a way to meet the tragedy of Neve's passing head-on. Honoring her memory near the spot where her death had occurred was in line with Neve's adventurous spirit and, to Giselle, a suitable send-off to her friend, wherever she landed next.

The site, which had a memorial cross, flowers and mementoes, was attended by several people who'd been closest to Neve and whose friendship Giselle had inherited as a result. These included Kimberly Herrington, a twenty-five-year-old artist who was just starting to make a name for herself in the local art scene; Seth Lombrozo, in his forties and a residential architect; Ethan Gladstone, a fiftysomething caterer; Jacinta Cruz, a thirty-year-old local documentary producer; Pablo Wersching, in his late forties and a dog-kennel owner; and Yuki Kotake, a fashion designer in her thirties. Some others Giselle didn't recognize, but she was happy to see that they were there to show the love and respect Neve so richly deserved.

Noticeably absent was Trooper Quincy Lankard. Giselle wondered if he had forgotten the time. Or had he ever truly intended to attend the vigil? Perhaps something else had come up, she considered while holding a candle in memory of her friend.

"Hey." Giselle heard the deep, recognizable voice over her shoulder. She turned to face Quincy Lankard, who locked eyes with her. He was dressed casually in a dark red pocket polo shirt, slim jeans and black Chelsea boots. His short dark hair was on full display and was parted on the side.

"You came," she said happily.

"Yeah. I wanted to be here to pay my respects to Ms. Chenoweth, fully honoring the dead as she makes her way to the spirit world."

"Nice to know." Giselle imagined that this appreciation for the bridge between life and death was in his DNA. As it was in hers, to one degree or another. "I'm sure that Neve would welcome your appearance, Trooper Lankard."

"I'm not on duty. Please—call me Quincy," he insisted.

"Okay." She smiled at him. "So long as you call me Giselle."

"Deal." He stuck out a hand, inviting her to shake it. She obliged and felt a tingle as their palms pressed together. Had he felt this too? "Good to see you again, Giselle," he said equably, "albeit under sad circumstances."

"Yes, it is sad," she agreed, adding, "but it's also meant to be a joyous occasion to the extent it can be—to remember the amazing life Neve had, though cut short."

"Glad to be a part of it and representing the Alaska Department of Public Safety, albeit off the clock."

Giselle nodded, then they turned and watched as some of Neve's friends spoke about her. When it came around to Giselle, she, too, said kind words about her late friend and couldn't help but wonder why such accidents happened to good people. She supposed that this was simply one of life's cruelties. It could happen to anyone if they were in the wrong place at the wrong time. She could only be thankful that it appeared as though death had come quickly for Neve, so she hadn't been left to suffer.

All that was left was for Neve to be returned to her family in Syracuse for a proper burial.

QUINCY WAS ALWAYS MOVED when people gathered to pay their respects to a fallen friend. Or family member. He'd certainly been there more times than he cared to admit on both fronts. As an AST, part of the community and a relative. He recalled losing his grandfather, Thayer Lankard, when Quincy had only been ten years old. Heart attack that his grandfather had never seen coming till it had been too late to prevent.

Then there was losing his best friend from high school, Grant Sackett, who'd died when his motorcycle had flipped on a dirt road. He'd been just twenty-two years old at the time.

But as Quincy watched the candlelight vigil for Neve Chenoweth and even said a few words in her memory as an outsider who was still able to feel the emotions that hung in the Alaska air like a dark cloud, he had to admit that it was the chance to spend more time with Giselle that motivated him most to attend.

Aside from being a real looker who'd caught his eye from the start, she impressed him as someone he wouldn't mind getting to know better. If she were willing. And available. But at the moment, she was huddled with other friends of Neve's, commiserating over her tragic loss. Respectfully, Quincy chose to slip away quietly, knowing there would be another opportunity to see Giselle in the future while not wanting to take away from her need to grieve a death that appeared to be nothing more than a terrible accident.

He headed home and looked forward to confirming this when the autopsy report came out tomorrow. In the meantime, he was happy to be able to return to his place to chill, knowing that there was more to life than the demands of his job and its connotations that were not always pleasant. That included being able to look at himself in the mirror and feeling that he had a hell of a lot to offer someone who wanted to join him in whatever journey lay ahead. Giselle suddenly entered his thoughts in that regard. He was aware that was putting the cart ahead of the horse but had no problem with fantasizing about it.

Quincy pulled up to his four-acre wooded property on Keystone Lane. The residence itself was a two-story, four-bedroom log home with a Kenai River frontage. He had purchased it five years ago, once it had become clear to him that he would likely be based in Soldotna for as long as he wished. Living there alone was another story altogether, and one he wanted to rectify sooner than later with a family to share it with.

He left his vehicle and headed inside the house. Spacious with an open concept, most of the features were solid wood, including a plank vaulted ceiling and maple hardwood flooring. A combination of double-hung and picture windows were everywhere, with woven wood shades. There was a gas fireplace in the great room, along with log furniture, and the midcentury-modern kitchen had a quartz epoxy countertop and contemporary appliances.

Quincy went to the kitchen and grabbed a can of beer from the stainless-steel refrigerator. He opened it and took a drink before checking his phone. There was a text message from his sister, Olivia. She was reminding him that his nephew Todd's fifth birthday was next week—in case he wanted to buy him a birthday present.

Quincy laughed. *Talk about pressure*, he thought with amusement. He loved Todd as his own son. Of course, he was happy to continue to spoil him, along with his six-year-old sister, Krista. At least as long as there were no kids of his own to dote over instead.

It occurred to Quincy that a couple of children's books would make a perfect birthday gift for Todd. He wondered what Giselle could recommend. If nothing else, it would give him an excuse to see her again, with the nature of Neve Chenoweth's death more or less a done deal.

He texted Olivia back, assuring her that he hadn't forgotten his nephew's birthday, before finishing off the beer and heading upstairs for a shower.

JUST DOWN THE Kenai Spur Highway on Angler Drive, in the Kenai Peninsula Borough of Alaska, sat an isolated one-story, two-bedroom farmhouse nestled in a wooded area, separated from nosy neighbors. At least this was how Justin Buckner saw it, making it the perfect location for him to set up shop as part of his plans. He had rented the place a little more than a week ago, after discovering at long last just where his ex-fiancée, Giselle Kinard, had ended up.

It had taken him almost three years to find her. Might have been sooner, but she had apparently just managed to elude him for parts unknown when he had tracked her to Oakland, California.

Damn her.

He walked back and forth across the worn hardwood flooring as if nothing better to do. The place had come furnished with rustic furniture and had picture windows. It was a far cry from his old spacious waterfront digs that had been a good fit. Till she'd left and everything had fallen apart.

He'd lost everything dear to him, starting with Giselle. His business had gone up in flames, figuratively and quite literally, and he was up a creek without a paddle. He'd had to get out of Dodge and do whatever he needed to keep his head above water.

And all with one central goal—get back what was owed him. That began with Giselle. She would pay dearly for leaving him high and dry. But not before others in her orbit paid the ultimate price first. Such as the pretty hiker he'd pushed to her death. And had made it appear to be an accident.

Just as he'd promised Giselle, should she ever decide to bolt and keep him from marrying her and having the life with her that he'd fantasized about for the past three years.

Drip. Drip. Drip.

One deadly step at a time.

He would save her for last. Make her sweat. And sweat. And worse.

Then finish her off—watching with satisfaction as her life was taken away.

Only then could he reclaim his own life and find someone else worthy of him to share it with.

Justin smoked the weed he was holding, feeling its nice effects as they worked their way into his system while continuing to pace. He thought about his ex-fiancée, his thick brows knitting with resentment. Revenge was on his mind.

Couldn't come soon enough. But patience was necessary, even against his eagerness to get this over with. Some things couldn't be rushed. This was one of them. Especially when playing with her psyche was so satisfying in and of itself.

Payback was a bitch, as the saying went.

Giselle would get the full brunt of it. Before she breathed her own last breath. Just like his previous ex, Jenna Sweeney, after she'd crossed him. And hadn't lived to talk about it for very long. He'd made sure she'd been put somewhere that they could never find her.

Justin took another puff on the joint and laughed as dark thoughts filled his head naughtily.

Chapter Three

Giselle was up bright and early for a Tuesday-morning jog on the empty street. She was wearing a purple cap and light summertime jogging clothes with white sneakers. Running was one of her favorite pastimes that she had continued when relocating to Taller's Creek.

I can't let Justin rob me of everything precious in my life, Giselle told herself stubbornly as she spied a moose in the short distance, seeming just as observant of her. It was but one of the fascinating things she had become accustomed to experiencing since moving to Alaska.

Though she could hardly say the same thing about Quincy Lankard, Giselle admittedly liked what she'd seen of the trooper thus far. Unfortunately, before she could've maybe tapped into that a bit more last night, he had disappeared from the candlelight vigil without even saying goodbye. Had that been his way of letting her know that he had fulfilled his obligation to Neve, assuming he saw it in that regard? Or had he bowed out gracefully out of respect to her and so as not to overstay his welcome among those who'd known her friend?

I'm probably overthinking it, Giselle thought as she rounded the corner and headed back to the apartment.

She would like to become better acquainted with Quincy, but only if she could do so without seeming over eager. Or having him pry too much into her past life, which she was in no hurry to have to relive. At least the parts that had anything to do with her ex-fiancé.

When she got inside the apartment, Muffin wasted little time in cozying up to her, obviously looking for some attention. "Okay, you win," she told the kitten, scooping her up into her arms and cradling her. "But only for a minute or two," she warned, knowing she needed to get ready for work. Muffin seemed more than happy to take what she could get, closing her eyes and purring happily.

An hour later, Giselle was in the bookstore putting up a display for a new science-fiction title with sales associate Ellen Ebsen. In her midtwenties and rail thin with long natural red hair in an A-line cut and big blue eyes, Ellen was vivacious and totally smitten with her girlfriend, Tatiana, whom she couldn't stop talking about.

"She's such a good person and makes me feel good about myself," Ellen gushed as she lined up a stack of books perfectly on the table.

"That's nice to hear," Giselle said enviously. She could only dream about having someone in her own life who could accept her for who she was rather than try to make her into someone else. Or threaten to ruin her life if she didn't capitulate.

"Does he want to come in or not?" Ellen asked, making a face.

Giselle looked at her, confused. "Who?"

"The man gawking in the window."

Facing that direction, Giselle's heart skipped a beat as she caught sight of a tall male who turned away at that moment. But not before she got a glimpse of his face. She recognized it. Or at least thought she did.

Justin? a voice in her head rang loudly. Had he found her? At last?

"What's wrong?" Ellen asked, concern in her tone. "You look like you've just seen a ghost!"

It might be better if I did, Giselle thought, unnerved. The dead couldn't hurt you. She blinked and then looked at the window again. The man was gone. Had it just been her imagination that it was Justin instead of someone simply innocently checking out the bookstore? That imagination had gone off the charts on different occasions during her time away from Justin.

Would he really look exactly the same way after three years? Like the face emblazoned in her memory as if seared there permanently, along with the sandy-colored, wavy hair in a midlength cut?

If Justin was truly in Taller's Creek, Giselle was sure he wouldn't hesitate to make his presence known as part of his sick process of tormenting her. Wouldn't he?

She regarded Ellen and admitted, "I thought I saw someone I recognized from among the living." Giselle twisted her lips thoughtfully. "But I was apparently mistaken."

"Happens to us all." Ellen shrugged indifferently. "Guess he decided not to come in after all and see if there was a book or two he might have been interested in."

"Guess not." Giselle glanced again at the window, wondering if the man might have rematerialized. Nothing doing. She supposed he'd just been passing by and might have only looked inside the bookstore haphazardly before going on his way. As for Justin, he was most likely still in Chesapeake, probably having charmed some other vulnerable woman to obsess over as his prospective bride or current wife.

Giselle tried to erase the thought out of her mind as they finished putting the display together and moved on to other duties.

JUSTIN COULD ALMOST feel the fear inside Giselle as she'd spotted him checking her out through the bookstore window. It was his intention to shake up his ex-fiancée a bit, mess with her pretty head as one step in the ultimate punishment she had coming to her. But before she could truly come to grips with the notion that what she was seeing wasn't merely a figment of her warped imagination but the real deal, he quickly averted his face and moved away from the window and out of her view.

Justin laughed with self-satisfaction as he moved briskly down the sidewalk. He wasn't about to make this exercise in terror easy for Giselle. Let her sweat it out. And sweat some more. Till she was dripping with perspiration and a fast-beating heart. That was the least of what she deserved for dropping out of his life, catching him off guard, leaving him wanting for much more from his ex than what he'd been given from her.

And he would have it. This wasn't the end of it. Not by a long shot. But he was clever enough to get under her skin while maintaining a low profile. Till it was time to make his presence felt again.

Until then, he was more than content to see just what it was that had drawn Giselle to Alaska. And Taller's Creek, in particular.

Justin chuckled musingly and crossed the street to get to his car.

QUINCY WAS STANDING over his desk as he read the autopsy report from the Alaska Department of Health State Medical Examiner's Office on Neve Chenoweth. According to Chief Medical Examiner Rhonda Ullerup, MD, Ms. Chenoweth had died as a result of an epidural hematoma caused by her head hitting a large rock. The death was ruled as accidental.

That didn't come as a surprise to Quincy, having expected as much. Still, part of him couldn't help but wonder if an experienced hiker with a military background would be so careless as to allow herself to trip or fall with a fatal outcome. Of course, the alternative was that her death had been due to other circumstances. Suicide seemed to be all but ruled out, with no indication that she'd been suffering from depression or PTSD. There was no reason to expect foul play. Till there was one.

"Sorry for her loved ones," remarked Alaska Bureau of Investigation Trooper Alan Edmonston, who had handed him a copy of the report. Alan, who was in his early forties, tall and solidly built with blue eyes and shaven bald beneath his campaign hat, shrugged resignedly. "It happens..."

"I'm sorry too." Quincy sighed, hating to admit that this type of thing in Alaska was par for the course, for better and far too often worse. "At least I'll be able to give them some closure," he reasoned. That included Giselle, whom he found himself wanting to get past this as quickly as possible. So that they might be able to have a do-over in getting to know each other, without Neve's tragic death hanging over them.

"That's all we can do," Alan said. "While being grateful we get to do this, go home ourselves and live to see another day."

"At least you have someone to go home to," Quincy remarked, knowing that Alan had been happily married to his high school sweetheart, Minnie, for two decades and counting. But this was hardly the time for Quincy to start feeling sorry for himself. He had too many blessings to count for that. And at least one prospect over the horizon.

"Your time will come," Alan told him, as though without a doubt. "In the meantime, enjoy your freedom while you can. Don't rush it, in spite of all the joy that comes with marriage."

Quincy wasn't quite sure how to interpret his words. "I'll try to remember that," he said, while more than willing to hedge his bet for marriage and family over the lonely life of a bachelor.

They talked briefly about a case of attempted assault in the process of a robbery that Alan was investigating while Quincy awaited his next assignment, before he headed out for Taller's Creek Books. There he planned to update Giselle on the official cause of Neve Chenoweth's death. And take the time as well to pick up some books for his nephew's birthday gift.

HE FOUND THE lovely woman he was looking for pointing a petite, red-headed female teenager in the right direction before Quincy watched Giselle take note of him standing there.

"Hey," he said, offering her a crooked grin.

"Hey." She smiled back softly and lost this as Giselle uttered inquiringly, "Where did you go last night? One moment you were there—the next you were gone…"

"I could see that you were pretty busy with the vigil, and I didn't want to intrude upon that, so I slipped away." Now Quincy wondered if that had been a mistake.

"You weren't intruding," she insisted, while admitting, "but I was caught up in the moment, so I completely understand why you left. Thanks for showing up, anyway."

"I was happy to do so." He met her eyes coolly. "In fact, one of the reasons I'm here now is to let you know that the autopsy report came in on Neve."

Giselle's thin brows lifted tensely. "Oh…?"

Without going into the morbid details, Quincy said, "As expected, it was concluded that the death was an accident." He watched what appeared to be relief wash across Giselle's face.

"I'm glad to know that it wasn't the result of something nefarious."

He cocked a brow curiously. "Did you think it could have been?"

"No," she spoke hastily. "It's just nice to have the cause of Neve's death official."

Quincy decided to take her word for it, even if he sensed there might have been something more to the story. "Okay."

Giselle eyed him interestedly. "You said that was one of the reasons you came to the bookstore. Was there another?"

To see you again, he told himself in all candor but responded smoothly, "Yes, my nephew, Todd, will turn five next week. Thought I'd pick up a few books for a birthday present. And while I'm at it, may as well grab some books for my six-year-old niece, Krista, so she doesn't feel left out. I was hoping you could recommend some?"

Giselle's eyes lit up. "Of course. I'd be happy to help you out there," she gushed.

Quincy followed her to the children's section, where Giselle presented him with a number of great choices, leaving it up to him to make the final decision on which books to purchase. After he did just that and paid Giselle for them, he got down to what was really on his mind, asking her, "So, are you seeing anyone these days?"

She appeared caught off guard by the question, making him wonder if it was wholly inappropriate, but she recovered quickly, stating, "Actually, I'm not." She paused, musing. "Are you?"

He grinned. "I'm pretty single at the moment—never been married either." *Maybe that could change on both fronts*, he thought, feeling even more emboldened. "Would you like to grab a bite to eat sometime?"

Giselle gazed at him encouragingly. "I'm on lunch break in ten minutes. We can grab a bite at the café across the street, if you're game?"

"Definitely," he told her without preface. "I'll go get us a table and wait for you."

"All right." She smiled genuinely. "See you in a few."

Quincy tipped his hat to that effect and walked off, looking forward to delving more into the woman behind the beautiful face.

Giselle was admittedly a little nervous as she entered Juanita's Café. She hadn't been on a real date in longer than she cared to remember. Was this a date? Or more of a friendly lunch?

She took a *wait and see* approach on that, welcoming the opportunity to get to know the ABI investigator better as Giselle spotted Quincy at a table by the window and was waved over.

He stood as she approached, sporting a handsome grin. "Hey."

"Hi." She smiled back, noting he had taken his hat off and put it on a corner of the table.

"I took a chance and ordered us both lattes," he said confidently.

"A latte is good," she voiced her approval as they both sat across from each other and Giselle took a sip of the drink.

"So, what's good on the menu?" Quincy asked, correctly presuming that she was a regular there.

She had no trouble responding. "The halibut sandwich is great and comes with coleslaw."

"Sounds good to me," he said, and they both ordered.

A short while later, they were eating and Giselle was still trying to decide what to say and what not to regarding her past life when, as expected, Quincy said curiously, "I'm guessing that you're not from Alaska?"

She laughed. "Is it that obvious?"

He laughed back. "No, but most people I run into seem to have relocated here from elsewhere, for one reason or another. Apart from that, I'm picking up a mid-Atlantic accent. Correct me if I'm wrong."

"You're not," Giselle confessed, impressed, though she had long believed she had no accent at all. "I'm from Virginia," she told him simply.

"Ahh." Quincy nodded satisfyingly as he bit into his sandwich. "Where in Virginia?"

I knew he would go there, Giselle thought. Had he been to the state? "Chesapeake," she responded, feeling comfortable enough to do so with him.

"Long ways from home," he commented. "How did you end up in Taller's Creek, if you don't mind my asking?"

"I don't," Giselle decided, without going into uncomfortable details. "After breaking up with my ex-fiancé three years ago, I felt a change was in order."

Quincy cocked a brow. "You were engaged?" he interjected before she could finish her thoughts.

"Yes." She didn't shy away from this now that she had chosen to mention that much. She hoped he didn't view this as a negative somehow. "Seemed like the right thing at the time—till I realized it would never have worked in the long run for many different reasons." She paused considerately. "Anyway, after bouncing around for a bit, I wound up in Alaska, which seemed interesting. With no other strong ties holding me back, I figured, why not?" She knew it wasn't quite that simple but wasn't ready to go there just yet, if ever. "I've been in Taller's Creek for a year and a half. It suits me."

"I can see that." Quincy peered at her admiringly. "Well, however it went down, I'm glad you're here."

"Thanks." Giselle blushed. "How about you? I'm guessing that you grew up in Alaska?"

"Good guess." He smiled again and dug his fork into the coleslaw. "Yeah, I've been here my entire life," he said matter-of-factly. "I'm a member of the Native Village of Eyak, an Alaska Native tribe."

"Cool," she said, piqued to learn more about his heritage later. "How long have you been with the Alaska State Troopers?"

"For about a decade now. Or since I've been out of college." Quincy took another bite of his sandwich. "It's been interesting, to say the least."

"I'm sure it has been." Giselle smiled as she imagined what type of cases and persons he must have come across in his line of work. "You've probably encountered a little of everything," she deduced, finishing off her coleslaw.

"Yeah, you could say that," Quincy conceded. "Some good, some not so much. Comes with the territory."

"I see." Giselle looked at him with a smile and wondered why some lucky woman hadn't already snatched him up. Maybe it was just because the right woman hadn't come into his life. Just as the right man hadn't come into hers. Certainly, that hadn't been the case with Justin. Far from it. Someone such as Quincy might be more to her liking. Or was she getting ahead of herself, his strong appeal notwithstanding?

"What other work have you done besides being an employee at a bookstore?" he asked knowingly, gazing at her.

Giselle sensed that he could see right through her, to some degree. She saw no reason to deflect from the truth in this instance. "I used to teach dance lessons after college," she told him evenly. "And also did my fair share of odd jobs to make ends meet, here and there." She felt her low lip quiver while considering the sacrifices she'd been forced to make in her life. "Anyway, I'm fine with being a bookstore sales associate at this point. As an avid reader, it gives me the opportunity to be around books."

"I like to read too, when afforded the time." Quincy dabbed his mouth with a napkin. "Mostly westerns, spy novels and some literary stuff."

"That's great," Giselle said, smiling. "I prefer historical novels, mysteries and cozies, but I'll pretty much read anything if it can hold my attention."

"Yeah, same here," he suggested and finished his latte.

She did the same while thinking that this was a nice start to opening herself up to the possibility of getting involved with someone again. Or at the very least, letting down her guard a bit after what Justin had put her through.

Before leaving the café, Giselle took the liberty of buying some freshly made blueberry cupcakes to pass out to the staff at the bookstore, knowing they would appreciate the gesture.

Quincy walked her across the street and said by the door of the bookstore, "It was nice hanging out with you."

"You too."

"Hope we can do it again sometime."

She smiled softly. "I'd like that."

He grinned at her. "Can I get your number?"

"Yes," she agreed. "Hand me your phone."

Quincy dug it out of his trousers and gave her the cell phone.

Giselle punched her number into his Contacts list. "There," she said, giving it back to him.

"Thanks," he said and called her. She grinned, taking the cell phone out of the back pocket of her linen pants. "Now you have my number, too."

She blushed. "Cool."

"Well, I've probably kept you long enough. I'll let you get back to it."

"All right." Giselle waited a beat while pondering whether or not to leave it at that. She decided to be courageous in wanting to see him again, sooner than later, tossing out, "Would you like to come to dinner—at my place?"

He didn't hold back in replying, "Sure. Just tell me when."

"How about tomorrow night at, say, seven?"

"I'll be there," he promised.

"I'll text you the address," she told him before they said their goodbyes.

Giselle went inside the bookstore feeling a mixture of excitement and nervousness in putting herself out there again after the disastrous experience she'd had with Justin, leaving her pessimistic where it concerned romance. But something told her that Quincy was cut from a whole different cloth and she had nothing to fear from him. And everything to look forward to.

Chapter Four

Giselle Kinard was still very much on Quincy's mind as he worked out at the Soldotna Gym on Kenai Spur Highway after work that evening. He'd enjoyed having lunch with her and getting to know more about her. He hoped to build on that now that they had a second date tomorrow. The fact that they had met under less-than-ideal circumstances wasn't as important as meeting at all and using this as a stepping stone to wherever it led. In his mind, that very well could be a magical place when all was said and done.

Quincy finished lifting weights as part of his routine for staying fit before heading to the treadmill, where he continued his workout. He was curious about Giselle once being engaged, sensing there was more to the story, but would leave it up to her to reveal in her own time if she wanted to. His main takeaway from it was the *better safe than sorry* suggestion he'd read in her words. Though he'd never come close to walking down the aisle with anyone as of yet, he'd been around and dated long enough to know that using instincts to avert disaster was the best way to go in the long run. Whatever had gone wrong between Giselle and her ex-fiancé, Quincy was just glad that she happened to be available here and now, as he was, and would go from there.

After finishing the exercise session, he took off his sweaty workout clothes, showered and put on his uniform in the locker room before heading to his car and an empty house to go to.

ON WEDNESDAY MORNING, while on duty, Quincy got the word from the AST's Southcentral Area-wide Narcotics team about a suspected bootlegging operation at a house on Blanden Street in Taller's Creek and a raid about to go down. He headed to the scene as part of the overall investigation. Though the ABI's regional major crimes unit was principally focused on cases involving serious crime against persons—such as homicides, suicides, sexual assaults, robberies, officer-involved incidents where deadly force was used and suspicious or unexplained deaths—they also took very seriously any and all illicit trafficking of liquor in the state. Unfortunately this practice was all too common in Alaska these days, as far as Quincy was concerned, and could hardly be ignored, with bootlegging often correlating with crimes of violence and property crimes in the area.

He reached the destination and rendezvoused with other troopers and investigators from the Taller's Creek Police Department before the operation got underway. In executing search warrants for the two-story residence and two vehicles, a GMC Sierra 1500 AT4 and a Chevrolet Silverado 2500 HD, the team came away with more than they bargained for.

Along with seventy-five bottles of illegal alcohol, confiscated were five hundred counterfeit M30 fen-

tanyl pills, two-hundred-plus grams of methamphet-
amine, more than twenty firearms and an undetermined
amount of hard cash. An adult male and female, both in
their early thirties, were arrested without incident at the
residence and faced a slew of charges.

"That went well," Quincy remarked to a SCAN team
investigator after securing his weapon back in its holster,
in that they had put at least one bootlegging operation
out of business, with no one getting hurt in the process.

"Knock on wood," Kelly Reppun, fiftysomething and
nearly six feet tall with curly crimson hair, quipped.
"You never know what's around the next corner in this
line of work."

"I hear you." He eyed her in earnest. "Guess we'll all
have to cross that bridge when we get to it."

"Yeah, we will," she agreed with a smile as the successful raid began to wind down.

Quincy was happy to move on, heading toward his
vehicle, unsure what was next on his plate. He used
that ironic thought to contemplate his dinner date tonight with Giselle. Something told him that he would
love whatever she had planned for their meal. And just
maybe, if things went his way, there might even be dessert to one degree or another to savor.

WITH THE DAY OFF, Giselle spent much of it getting her
apartment in order. Not that it needed much cleaning up,
as she was always tidy. But sprucing it up just a bit for
her date with Quincy seemed like a good idea. Now she
was counting on Muffin, who could be finnicky around
strangers, to behave herself.

Hope he isn't allergic to cats, Giselle told herself,

not wanting there to be any unforeseen impediments to spending time with the trooper and seeing where it went. Before she headed out to the supermarket to pick up a few items for dinner, she lifted up Muffin and warned her playfully, "Now, you behave yourself this evening!"

Ten minutes later, Giselle was moving a cart down the aisle at Safeway grocery store on Kenai Spur Highway. She was gathering all she needed for a dinner that included baked salmon coated with chopped pecans, herbed garlic potatoes, fresh spinach, and blueberry-and-raspberry cream pie. Admittedly, she was excited at the prospect of preparing a meal for someone other than herself, which hadn't been the case very often since moving to Alaska.

Maybe this could become a whole new tradition, Giselle thought with a chuckle while wondering if she could measure up to what Quincy might have been used to eating. Perhaps as a single man, he was settling for takeout and fast food and hadn't had too many home-cooked meals himself of late.

When she switched to the section of the store that sold beer, wine and spirits, Giselle studied the wines, trying to guess if Quincy preferred red or white to wash down the food. She went with the white wine.

Just as she grabbed a bottle off the shelf, Giselle happened to look toward the end of the aisle. A tall man was standing there, peering at her, almost tauntingly.

Justin Buckner.

Without even realizing what she was doing till it was too late, the wine bottle slipped from Giselle's hands and crashed to the floor. The bottle shattered and, with it, the wine spilled everywhere.

As she gathered up the courage to do so, Giselle looked up, expecting her ex-fiancé to come barreling toward her like a battering ram to hurt her in any way he could.

Instead she was surprised to see that there was no one there. Where was he? Why hadn't he come after her?

Had she actually imagined seeing him? Or could this have been his way of psychologically terrorizing her?

"Ma'am, are you all right?"

The voice boomed in her ears, and Giselle turned to see a man standing there. He had a concerned look on his oblong face. His sandy-blond hair reminded her of Justin's. Even the face bore some resemblance to the person she had last seen three years ago. Could the man now before her have been the one she'd seen at the end of the aisle? Giselle realized now that he was wearing a store uniform and she had not bothered to home in on the clothing worn by the man she'd thought was Justin.

She cleared her throat and uttered embarrassingly, "I'm fine. Other than having butter fingers. The wine bottle slipped from my hand somehow…"

"That happens to the best of us," he said understandingly. "Don't worry about it. I'll get someone to clean this up."

"Thank you," Giselle told him but would definitely pay for the bottle of wine anyway. She grabbed a second bottle, this time determined to hang on to it, thanked the employee again for what she secretly now believed had been a case of mistaken identity and sidestepped the broken glass and wine as best she could before pushing her cart down the aisle.

Moving in the direction where she had imagined seeing Justin, Giselle's heart raced as she wondered if he might actually be waiting for her to emerge, so as to spring himself upon her. But when she reached the junction that was wider spaced and bordered multiple aisles, there was no sign of him.

Checking the aisle over on both sides, she was relieved to see that Justin was nowhere to be found. He hadn't somehow made his way to Taller's Creek, Alaska, to haunt her after all. The sooner she got this in her head—instead of allowing someone from her past to mess with it out of the blue—the better off she would be. And better her chances of finding romance with someone worthy of her.

Such as Quincy Lankard.

JUSTIN WAS TOYING with Giselle when he stood in front of the aisle where she was peering over bottles of wine as if they held the keys to the universe. He had followed her to the grocery store while being sure to keep his distance, so as not to spoil the mischievous fun just yet. He only wanted her to catch a glimpse of him, sure she would remember what he looked like—only to dash out of sight in the blink of an eye. Leaving her to second-guess that it was truly him, come to town to get his revenge, as promised.

It worked like a charm, as he overheard Giselle speaking with a male employee, whom Justin had spotted earlier and bore some resemblance to himself. Undoubtedly, she would assume this was the man Giselle thought she saw in the aisle. And not her worst nightmare. As he viewed himself.

Justin watched from behind a liquor display as Giselle scanned the store to see if she could spot him, apparently still not trusting herself that he had not, in fact, found her. But he wasn't quite ready just yet to give her the satisfaction—frightening as it would be—to know that she was right. When she seemed confident that he was nowhere to be found, he saw that she relaxed the strain in her pretty face and went on to pay for her wine.

He quickly exited the store, careful not to draw any attention to himself. Once outside, he breathed in the fresh Alaska air and went to his car, which he had paid for in cash.

After waiting for a few minutes, Justin spied Giselle coming out of the supermarket with her cart. She had parked her Honda CR-V just feet from his car. Her green eyes took a sweeping glance of the parking lot routinely— or perhaps hoping to spot him—but he ducked to be on the safe side. Once she got inside her car, he looked up and watched as she drove off.

He thought about following her but saw no need to tip his hand at this point. Besides, he knew exactly where she lived, having already scoped out the place more than once. When the time was right, he would be more than happy to make his presence felt, when she least expected it.

Justin started his car and began whistling the first song to pop into his head before driving off.

QUINCY HAD TO admit that he felt like he was in high school all over again when he'd had his first date with Mona Eubank. Though it had gone absolutely nowhere, the initial enthusiasm was the same. As he drove toward Giselle's apartment in his personal vehicle, he hoped for a more promising outcome. He'd even cleaned up nicely, if he said so himself, for the dinner date—wearing a yellow Oxford dress shirt, dark blue trousers and black loafers. It actually felt good to dress up a bit as part of spending time with someone he wanted to become better acquainted with.

Arriving at Giselle's apartment building, Quincy wondered briefly if he should have brought something along with him, like wine or whatever. He was admittedly out of practice in that regard.

Next time, he told himself optimistically as Quincy emerged from the gray Subaru Forester and headed to her first-floor unit.

It took only one ring of the bell before the door opened and Giselle's beautiful face appeared before him. "Right on time," she said enthusiastically.

Knowing he had arrived late for the candlelight vigil, Quincy was determined not to miss out on any moment they could spend together. "Wouldn't have it any other way," he joked.

She smiled. "You look nice."

"Thanks." He regarded her, wearing a body-flattering floral midi dress and espadrille wedge sandals, to go with her natural good looks, and Quincy had to say honestly, "You look even better."

"And thank you back." Giselle blushed. "Come in." He did so, and she said humbly, "This is home."

He gave the place a sweeping glance—taking in the modern though worn furniture in the living and dining room combo and small kitchen with a butcher-block countertop and slate appliances—noting everything neatly in place. "It's nice," he told her, while imagining Giselle fitting right in at his larger residence. Then movement on the floor caught his eye, and Quincy saw a Burmese kitten race along the baseboard.

"That's Muffin," Giselle said proudly.

"Hey, Muffin." He grinned at the kitten and, before she could ask, said, "I love cats. Had some when I was a boy—and dogs too."

"Cool." She flashed her teeth and watched as her kitten came toward Quincy before abruptly running away. "Muffin's unusually shy today," Giselle offered apologetically.

"I'm sure she'll come around once she sees I'm on her side—and yours," he spoke confidently.

"Good to know." Giselle smiled again. "Dinner's ready."

Quincy picked up the scent of food, prompting him to say, "Smells great."

"Hope you feel the same after eating," she teased.

"I'm sure I will," he countered perceptively. "What can I do?"

"You can open the wine, if you like." She eyed the bottle on the counter and wineglasses beside it.

"Sure thing." Quincy proceeded to do just that, while admiring her. When they literally bumped into each other in the kitchen, he felt a surge of sexual energy zip through him. Had she felt it too? He considered this as he poured the wine.

A couple of minutes later, they were sitting across from each other on cushioned chairs with oval backrests at the beveled wooden table.

"So, what do you think?" Giselle asked anxiously once Quincy had started eating.

After swallowing, he grinned, looked her straight in the eye and responded keenly, "It's delicious!"

Her features relaxed. "That's good to hear."

Quincy took it that she didn't cook very often. Or at least not for male guests. That made him feel special. A light that he was beginning to see her in too. "Do you have family in Chesapeake?" he wondered curiously.

"Not anymore." Giselle's expression dampened. "My parents both died not too long ago from illnesses. They never had any more children after I came along."

Quincy met her eyes sadly. "Sorry to hear about your folks."

"Do your parents live around here?" she asked.

"They live in Juneau," he answered matter-of-factly, slicing his knife into the baked salmon. "I try to visit whenever I can, but it's not often enough as far as they're concerned."

"I'm sure." Giselle smiled softly. She dug a fork into the herbed garlic potatoes. "I take it your nephew and niece live nearby?"

"Yeah, Todd and his sister, Krista, live in Nikiski, with my sister, Olivia, and her husband, Kenneth."

"Nice to know you can visit them at any time."

"True." Quincy lifted his wineglass and took a sip, regarding her thoughtfully. "You must miss home?" He assumed that was the case, even if she was clearly happy to put some distance between her and the ex-fiancé.

"I do, honestly," she responded, a catch to her voice. She colored. "But there was really nothing there for me anymore, so it was just a good time to move on…"

"I can respect that," he told her, even if thinking that there was more to the story that she wasn't revealing.

But he wasn't about to press for more, as Quincy was just grateful that she had made the move to Alaska—allowing them this opportunity to make a connection, as though it was meant to be.

"Are you ready for dessert?" Giselle got his attention.

"Absolutely." He finished off his meal, then helped her clear the table and bring over their slices of blueberry-and-raspberry cream pie, to go with more wine.

"So, aside from reading spy novels and westerns, what else do you like to do?" she asked inquisitively, putting the fork into her mouth.

He leaned back in the chair. "I enjoy hunting, fishing, kayaking, working out—the usual things for most Alaskans…"

"Nice." She smiled. "I've never hunted and have only gone fishing on occasion, but I have kayaked," she said. "I also love to swim, jog and hike…"

Quincy watched her shoulders slump and suspected she was thinking about the accidental death of her friend, Neve. "Those are all worthwhile pastimes," he said quickly and ate more of the pie.

"I agree." She sipped her wine.

They both saw Muffin walk into the room, study them curiously and, once satisfied, make her way toward the kitchen to finish off her own meal, causing them to chuckle.

Quincy mused about her career as a dance instructor and asked interestedly, "What type of dances did you teach?"

Giselle's eyes lit up as she answered coolly, "Ballroom, bolero, country western, foxtrot, hustle, rumba, salsa, tango, waltz—you name it."

He laughed. "Wow! Sounds like you taught every-thing."

She giggled. "Pretty much."

Quincy could tell that she missed dancing and was obviously good at what she did. So why not continue being a dance instructor in Alaska? Was there any reason, in particular, why she would turn her back on this for work at a bookstore?

Instead of asking her and risk being told it was none of his business, ruining the date, Quincy decided to take a different approach. He stood up and said, "I'm not much of a dancer, but if you're game, I'd love for you to show me a few moves..."

Giselle stared at the notion for a long moment or two before yielding to the challenge. She rose to her feet and said, "You're on."

Quincy watched as she grabbed her cell phone off the table and put on a jazz tune from her playlist; then Giselle took his hand and gave him a crash course in tango that morphed into a waltz. Both had them pressed together and holding each other, tapping into his libido.

"You're a natural at this," she declared, clearly in her own element.

"I'll take your word on that," he said soulfully while hoping not to step on her toes, literally, as Giselle had kicked off her sandals to dance barefoot.

Before he knew it, Quincy was kissing her. He wasn't quite sure who'd initiated the kiss. Only that Giselle's soft lips were a perfect fit for his. And vice versa. He probably could have kissed her and held her in his arms all night.

But before they went much further, Quincy did the

honorable thing in wanting to make sure this was really what she wanted, and neither would have any regrets—so he pulled back. If he played his cards right, there would be plenty of time to pick up where they'd left off.

Giselle seemed to be of the same mind as she touched her swollen lips and told him, "Thank you, Quincy, for...a very pleasant evening."

He nodded, gazing at her eyes intently. "Thanks for inviting me."

By the time he left, Quincy was already looking forward to spending more time with Giselle. And all that came with the desirous territory.

Chapter Five

Giselle was still on cloud nine the next morning as she got ready for work, with Muffin observing quietly. Quincy had kissed her as they'd been doing a tango-and-waltz combination dance. Or had it been the other way around? In any event, she'd enjoyed the feel of his lips upon hers. It had been a long time since she had kissed or been kissed by anyone, hesitant to move in that direction with the specter of Justin still hanging over her like a shroud.

But Quincy had singlehandedly managed to change that and resurrect in her the feelings of wanting to be with someone again. While giving Giselle hope that he might be that person, if things continued to progress in that direction. Or, at the very least, a man that she wanted in her life in Alaska.

After putting some whitefish-and-rice wet kitten food in a bowl for Muffin and watching her devour it, Giselle left the apartment, hopped into her car and drove off. Moments later, she spotted a lynx come out from a batch of yellow cedars. The wildcat seemed to look directly at her, perhaps more out of curiosity than anything, before heading back into the trees.

Upon reaching her destination and parking in the

back lot for employees, Giselle walked into the bookstore, where they had a book signing and reading by an Alaska Native author of young adult fiction scheduled for this afternoon.

Jill was standing by the checkout counter, along with Wesley. Both were admiring a dozen orange roses on a table. They turned when seeing her approaching.

"Hey," Giselle uttered uneasily. "What's with the roses?"

"Beats me," Jill said, shrugging her shoulders. "They were delivered here this morning. The card that came with them simply said, 'From a book lover.'"

"Seems to me someone has a secret admirer," Wesley suggested and held the bouquet to his nose. He eyed Giselle suspiciously. "Who do you think the lucky person is?"

"I have no idea," she answered with a snap, trying hard to maintain her composure. In fact, Giselle did have some idea. Or at least was no stranger herself to orange roses. Justin had loved giving them to her as a symbol of his hold on her, desire for her and enthusiasm for the forever relationship he'd envisioned them having. Initially she'd thought it was the sweetest thing and indicative of what at the time had seemed to be a reflection of what they could become as a couple.

But soon, she'd grown to detest the orange roses, for they'd become symbolic of his obsession with her and his brazen attempt to control her at all costs. Whatever it had taken.

Could Justin have sent the roses to let her know he was in Taller's Creek? And that she had not imagined seeing him at the bookstore window—and later at the grocery store?

The mere notion sent chills up and down Giselle's spine. Even as she tried to assess the likelihood that her ex-fiancé had managed to locate her after three years away from him.

"They smell so good," gushed Sadie, who had joined the group. In her early twenties and a marine biology major at the Kenai Peninsula College in Soldotna, she worked only two days a week for some extra income.

Giselle watched as Sadie, who was tall and thin with black hair in a lob with faux bangs, put her nose to the orange roses. "Yes, they do," she agreed from memory of the fruity fragrance.

"Whose are they?" Sadie asked, her bold blue eyes flashing.

"Apparently the bouquet is for all of us," Jill declared.

"I'll go along with that," Wesley said. "I suppose they were simply meant to brighten our day collectively."

"Maybe," Giselle muttered, mainly to herself, as she wondered if the roses were much more ominous in their intentions than any of the others could ever imagine. She contemplated the thought as they spread out to get to work.

JUSTIN DID FIFTY PUSH-UPS on the well-worn hardwood floor in his rental home, straining his muscles to the limit but determined to do so. He figured that by now, Giselle had already laid eyes on the bouquet of orange roses that he'd had delivered before she'd arrived at work. He had little doubt that it had gotten under her skin and made her pretty uncomfortable. Surely she hadn't forgotten that it had been his flower of choice to give her as an indication of his love and cherishing the long-term relationship he'd envisioned for them?

I don't think so, Justin told himself confidently as he passed the fifty mark and decided to do fifty more push-ups. He sucked in a deep breath and thought some more about his ex-fiancé. She might have bailed on him, but it would come at a huge price for her and those within Giselle's orbit. He would see to that, and then some.

Justin considered his latest step in that direction. The window was starting to close on his still gorgeous ex.

And there was nothing she—or anyone else—could do about it. He would have his revenge and had no intention of stopping what she had started until he did what was necessary to make things right.

QUINCY FOUND HIMSELF daydreaming about kissing Giselle yesterday but put that thought on hold as dispatch reported that a Taller's Creek woman had been found dead at her house by her sister, with the deceased having apparently shot herself. If true, the mere thought of someone taking her own life—particularly in such a gruesome fashion as what a bullet could do to the body—whatever the reason might have been, shook Quincy. Just as it did when any life was lost unnecessarily.

That included the accidental death of Giselle's friend, Neve Chenoweth.

He felt grateful that it hadn't been Giselle instead, as Quincy didn't want to see anything come between her and him in seeing what the future might have in store for them.

Conferring with his boss at the ABI Soldotna Major

Crimes Unit, Lieutenant Ron Valdez, Quincy passed along the latest disturbing incident. "Possible suicide," he told him bleakly as they stood in the hall.

Valdez, pushing sixty, of medium build and six feet tall, with gray hair in a Caesar cut, narrowed brown eyes and muttered, shaking his head forlornly, "When will they ever learn that there's always another way to go?"

"Never soon enough," Quincy only wished he didn't have to say, but so true. As he knew the lieutenant was well aware of, after tragically losing his daughter, Margie, from Valdez's first marriage, to suicide five years ago. "I'm on my way to check it out."

Valdez nodded, and then Quincy gave him a brief update on an earlier case before heading over to Taller's Creek.

QUINCY ARRIVED AT the single-story cabin on Lenbrooke Avenue and was greeted by Taller's Creek PD Sergeant Miriam Fontaine, who had requested the ABI's assistance.

"Sergeant," he acknowledged casually while regarding the thirtysomething first responder. She was blue eyed and muscular in her uniform, with dark hair in a midlength cut. A Glock 22 40 S&W caliber service pistol sat in an open-carry waistband holster.

"Thanks for coming," she said routinely and made a face. "Looks like the victim may have died from a self-inflicted gunshot to the head. Her name is Yuki Kotake, a thirty-four-year-old fashion designer. The victim's sister, Willow Kotake, discovered the body—"

"That couldn't have been easy," Quincy muttered thoughtfully.

"When is it ever?" Miriam concurred drearily.

"Yeah." He paused. "Let's have a look…"

He followed her to the cabin while noting a white Subaru Outback and red Chevrolet Blazer in the gravel driveway along with a wooded backdrop.

Inside Quincy saw a young blond-haired female officer consoling a twentysomething slender Asian woman with short and curly brunette hair. She was bawling her brown eyes out as they sat on a black leather sofa, telling him everything he needed to know.

Or almost. He still needed to view the deceased and assess the situation.

"She's in the back room," Miriam told him.

Quincy headed across the blue carpeted floor and made his way down the hallway. He passed by a bedroom on the right and then a bathroom before arriving at the back bedroom. Stepping inside, he first took note of the platform bed that was unmade, then his eyes caught sight of the legs on the floor on the other side of the bed.

When he went around to that side, Quincy saw the victim lying flat on her back, her face turned sideways. Blood had streamed from a bullet wound to her temple, spilling onto long, straight black hair and the carpeting. She was wearing a green tank top, frayed flare jeans and was barefoot. A handgun lay near the body. He recognized it as a Walther PDP, or Performance Duty Pistol, 9mm Luger semiautomatic handgun and spotted a single shell casing against the wall.

Turning back to the deceased, Quincy studied her face further and did a double take, as it occurred to him only now that he had seen her before.

Picking up on his reaction, Miriam, who had followed him to the bedroom, asked, "What is it?"

"She was at a candlelight vigil a few days ago for Neve Chenoweth," he responded in almost disbelief.

"The hiker," Miriam said knowingly.

"That's the one." Quincy glanced at Yuki Kotake, whom he hadn't spoken to at the vigil, but Giselle had.

"Hmm. And now she's dead too…" Miram wrinkled her nose. "So sad."

"Yeah." He didn't disagree. But Quincy wondered if it went beyond that. Two friends—both of whom Giselle had known by extension—to die within days of each other. What were the odds? "The crime scene unit will process the scene," Quincy told her, both aware that any such death had to be treated with the possibility of foul play, no matter the presumed cause and nature of a death—with any physical evidence collected accordingly. "In the meantime, I'd like to talk to the victim's sister."

"Of course," Miriam agreed. "Officer Hutton can help you, if needed. Beyond that, the State Medical Examiner's Office should be here shortly to collect the body."

Quincy nodded and went back into the living room, where the officer was still trying her best to comfort the obviously distraught sister of Yuki Kotake. Though he certainly felt for her in that trying moment, what had to be done had to be done for the investigation.

Moving toward her, Quincy motioned to Officer Hutton that he needed to question Willow Kotake and watched as the officer nodded and gingerly rose up and stepped away from the young woman. Taking Hutton's place on the sofa, Quincy said softly, "I'm with the Alaska Bureau of Investigation. I'm very sorry for your loss. I need to ask you a few questions..."

Willow nodded with expectation, wiping away tears from her eyes. "I understand," she said in a shaky voice.

"How did you come to discover your sister... Ms. Kotake dead?"

"I was supposed to meet Yuki for lunch at a restaurant in Soldotna," Willow explained. "When she didn't show up or answer her cell phone, I drove over here, concerned." She wiped her nose. "I have a key to her house." Willow drew a breath. "I found Yuki in her bedroom—"

Quincy nodded respectfully. "Do you know if your sister owned a gun?"

"Yes, she purchased a gun last year for self-defense." Willow's voice dropped contemplatively. "I never thought it was a good idea."

"Was she being threatened by anyone?"

"Not that I'm aware of."

That aroused his curiosity, and all things considered, Quincy asked point-blank, "Was Ms. Kotake suicidal?"

Willow batted curly lashes, musing, then responded, "Yes, she has suffered from depression and had suicidal thoughts from time to time in her life, but she'd been taking antidepressants to control it."

"Was there something that happened recently that might have triggered shooting herself?" He needed to know.

She stared at the question for a second or two. "Last week Yuki and her boyfriend, Armand, broke up," Willow said. "They fought all the time... But Yuki still took the breakup hard and seemed to want to get back together with him, in spite of everything."

Quincy took this in. Had the attempt at reconciliation failed? Causing Yuki Kotake to take her own life? Or was there an even more ominous explanation for her death? Perhaps the ex-boyfriend had come to the cabin, used her handgun and killed Yuki in a fit of rage? Stranger things had happened in a state which had one of the highest murder rates in the entire country.

But he didn't want to get ahead of the curve in getting to the root of the fashion designer's untimely demise. At least not before the CSU investigation and autopsy were completed.

Also weighing on Quincy's mind was having to confront Giselle with yet another death of a friend in short order while wondering how she would take it.

THE BOOK SIGNING EVENT went without a hitch, as the teen-fiction bestselling author Charlotte Hawk held her seated audience captive while she read the first chapter of her new novel about an Alaska Native girl's life in Alaska during the 1930s. Giselle admired the talented writer who looked like she was barely older than a teenager herself, with soft features and frizzy raven hair in a long fishtail French braid, though she was in her early thirties.

Maybe someday I'll try writing a novel, Giselle told herself dreamily, figuring that between her love for fiction and life's experiences, good and bad, anything was possible. She even imagined coauthoring a book with Quincy, combining what each brought to the table, should things between them progress accordingly.

As Charlotte wrapped things up by signing every copy of her book that they had available and was quickly

ushered out the door by her publicist for another scheduled event, Quincy was coming into the bookstore. He
smiled at the author for whom he had something in
common with as Native Alaskans, and Giselle felt the
slightest twinge of jealousy, though she knew it was inappropriate, if not wholly unfounded. She had no right
to feel the need to want to command all his attention.
What was meant to be between them would occur naturally and without insecurities by either of them. Unlike
in her last toxic relationship with Justin.

"Hey." Quincy's voice was even as he came up to her.

"Hey." Giselle looked up at him, feeling foolish for
such silly thoughts, even as the kiss and dance they'd
shared yesterday evening flashed brightly in her head.

He met her eyes solemnly. "You have a minute?"

"Yes." She sensed that there was something serious
on his mind. "Why don't we step outside?" Giselle suggested, knowing she could spare a few minutes without
being missed now that the bookstore had all but emptied
with the Charlotte Hawk signing over.

"All right," Quincy agreed and followed her back out
the door.

"What is it?" she almost hated to ask, ill at ease.

"Something bad has happened," he began delicately,
"and I wanted you to hear it from me…" He sighed. "Another friend of yours, Yuki Kotake, is dead."

"What? Yuki…dead?" Giselle swallowed thickly.
"How?"

"It appears as though she shot herself to death," Quincy
said straightforwardly. "Her sister, Willow, discovered the
body at Ms. Kotake's cabin." He paused. "I'm sorry—"

Giselle felt the color drain from her face. How could Yuki be dead, so soon after Neve?

Don't test me, Giselle!

The stark warning from Justin registered in her head.

If you even think about ever leaving me, Giselle, just know that you'll pay for it in ways you can't even imagine. I'll go after everyone you care about...or cares about you, even a little...one by one. Saving you for last.

Was this Justin's way of following through on his wicked promise? Had he somehow been involved in Yuki's and Neve's deaths, in spite of the evidence and appearances to the contrary? The mere possibility had Giselle freaking out.

"What's wrong?" Quincy asked, peering at her with concern.

Giselle forced herself to meet his steady gaze and uttered unevenly, "I think my ex-fiancé may have something to do with Yuki's death...and maybe Neve's too..."

Chapter Six

Quincy had admittedly been thrown for a loop when hearing Giselle suggest that her ex-fiancé could have been a killer of not one but two of her friends. How could she believe such a thing? Or did she know something he didn't that could somehow defy logic as well as what was generally believed to be true in the deaths of both Yuki Kotake and Neve Chenoweth?

"Care to explain?" Quincy demanded after Giselle had asked him to pause that thought till they were seated at a table at the café across the street with cups of black coffee in front of them.

She tasted the coffee thoughtfully, then said ill at ease, "I haven't been entirely forthcoming about my ex..." She drew a breath. "His name is Justin Buckner. To say that we had a contentious relationship would be a serious understatement. Justin was possessive, controlling, jealous, mean spirited, manipulative and very vindictive, as it turned out."

Giselle sipped more coffee, and Quincy felt her anguish and wanted nothing more than to comfort her. He still needed to hear just where this was going. "I'm listening," he prodded gingerly.

She sighed and continued, "I couldn't take it—him—anymore and… I ran away—"

"Ran away?" Quincy gazed at her.

"Yes." Nodding, Giselle stammered, "I was fearful of what he would do if I broke things off—or, worse, stayed and kept taking everything he was dishing out—and what I might have done in needing to defend myself or break the stranglehold he had on my life. Three years ago, not trusting the police or a restraining order to protect me, I just got up and left my entire life behind without looking back. I moved around the mainland for a while, going from one state to the next, always looking over my shoulder, knowing he would never let me go. Not without exacting some sort of retaliation that I didn't even want to imagine…" She sucked in a deep breath. "I ended up in Alaska, where I thought I might finally be free of him. Now I have to wonder if Justin has reemerged to make my life hell. And other unsuspecting lives as well."

Quincy took a moment to let this sink in. Especially the part about hiding in Alaska—Taller's Creek—from her ex-fiancé. Was it her plan to eventually head back to Chesapeake, Virginia? Was she really from there? Or was that also part of her subterfuge in staying one step ahead of an abusive and otherwise creep of a former boyfriend?

I can't allow my personal feelings of how this might impact the long-term potential between us to get in the way of the ordeal this man has obviously put Giselle through, Quincy mused as he put the coffee mug up to his lips. More important at the moment was why she would believe that her ex-fiancé could have anything to do with two local deaths that gave no indication there was foul play involved.

"I wish you had told me about the situation with your ex in relation to your living in—or hiding out— in Taller's Creek," Quincy couldn't help but say against his better judgment.

"I know," Giselle owned up to, clutching her mug of coffee. "I'm sorry I wasn't up front about that." She frowned, sipping the coffee. "It's not exactly the type of thing I wanted to share with anyone," she stressed. "I've been trying my best to put that dark part of my past behind me. I hope you can understand that."

"I can," he admitted, having seen firsthand in the course of his work with the ABI that domestic violence and psychological abuse and manipulation was real and came in many forms. Law enforcement and restraining orders, if that came at all, could only go so far against a determined aggressor. Sometimes escaping the situation was the only viable remedy in order to survive it. Clearly Giselle had reached this breaking point and done what she'd felt she'd needed to do. He could hardly criticize her for that, even if the protector in Quincy would have wanted to be there for her from the start and every step along the way.

"Thank you," Giselle uttered softly.

"So, what makes you think this Justin Buckner could be responsible for Yuki Kotake's death?" Quincy cocked a brow curiously. "Much less Neve Chenoweth's death?"

Giselle sighed, pondering it for a long moment. "Justin warned me that if I ever left him, he would find me and make me pay," she said nervously. "His exact words were, 'If you even think about ever leaving me,

Giselle, just know that you'll pay for it in ways you can't even imagine. I'll go after everyone you care about…or cares about you, even a little…one by one. Saving you for last.'" She waited a beat and continued, "With two people in my orbit suddenly dead within days of one another, I'm left to wonder if Justin—even after three long years apart—has somehow found a way to do what he promised…before coming after me."

Quincy leaned forward with a jaundiced eye. "Have you seen Buckner in Taller's Creek?"

"Not exactly…" Giselle confessed.

Quincy arched a brow. "What does that mean?"

"It means that I thought I saw him once, looking in the window of the bookstore," she responded. "But then the person was gone. Another time, I thought Justin was standing at the end of an aisle at the beer, wine and liquor area at Safeway." She flushed. "But apparently it was only a store employee who resembled Justin. Or at least how I remembered he looked from three years ago. Also, someone left a dozen orange roses at the bookstore." Giselle sighed. "Though the card with them was only signed 'From a book lover,' Justin often gave me a dozen orange roses when we were together…"

"Hmm…" Quincy's tone was laced with skepticism about her ex being in town. And having anything to do with the deaths of her friends. "It doesn't exactly sound as though what you've said amounts to real proof that Buckner is in town stalking you…or worse—"

"I know. Silly, right?" Giselle flushed sheepishly. "Guess I've just allowed my imagination to run wild lately." She wrinkled her nose. "Still, even with that, I'm scared that he could have discovered my whereabouts…

and he's definitely capable of inflicting bodily harm on anyone who crossed him. Especially me—"

Quincy sat back, mulling over her position and apparently valid concerns. Though she had not unquestionably laid eyes on her ex—but rather seemed to have made herself believe she had seen him—it didn't seem like something that could be dismissed. Even if she *was* mistaken. Given her difficult—and frankly, disturbing— history with the man, Quincy in no way held that against Giselle. She was only human, and it was understandable that Buckner's image would manifest itself from time to time. Or even likely misconstruing someone innocently sending flowers to the bookstore as coming from him.

But it wasn't the same thing as actually seeing her ex-fiancé in the flesh.

"So, what does Buckner do for a living?" Quincy wondered, hoping to gain some perspective as it related to his ability to travel without being missed.

"Justin's a financial planner," Giselle answered. "At least he was at the time I broke away from him."

"In Chesapeake?" Quincy regarded her questioningly, assuming she had been on the level about this part of her past.

"Yes." She met his eyes squarely. "It's where we met," she replied.

"Okay—just checking," he sought to justify his asking. "I'd be happy to look into whether or not Justin Buckner could actually be in Alaska—Taller's Creek— currently or if he has been at any time recently," Quincy volunteered, knowing that putting the notion to rest, more or less, by indicating this likely wasn't the case would give her peace of mind, if nothing else. Never mind that this might be guesswork at best, all things considered, unless Buckner was a wanted man or otherwise making it easy to track his movements.

"Thank you." Giselle's strained features relaxed ever so slightly.

"That being said, the chance that Buckner played a role in either of the deaths of your friends seems small at best," Quincy reiterated. "As we've already discussed, Neve Chenoweth's death was ruled an accident. And as things now stand, it appears that Yuki Kotake took her own life. There's no indication to the contrary, pending an examination of the firearm used, gunshot residue and the autopsy on the deceased."

"I guess I'll have to accept that," she said, running a finger along the rim of her mug. "Unless you find out otherwise."

"All right." Quincy flashed a faint smile, while recognizing that, Buckner aside, Giselle had still lost two acquaintances tragically. No sugarcoating that. Still, accidents happened. So did suicide. In this instance, both would be somewhat easier to accept than either woman being a victim of homicide. "Well, I'd better let you get back to the bookstore," he said, even if part of him would rather they spent more time together with a fresh start now that everything was out in the open with her true reasons for being in Alaska. He could only hope that she was there to stay and would not find herself running away from him.

"Probably a good idea." Giselle nodded musingly. "The last thing I need is to get fired for an unauthorized extended break."

"Wouldn't want that." *Especially if it means giving*

you a reason to go elsewhere, Quincy thought. He stood, watching her do the same. "I'll walk you back."

GISELLE WAS RUNNING *for her life. Her pursuer was intent upon making sure she never saw another day, so consumed was he to have her at all costs. Or see to it that she paid a price that there was no walking back from.*

But it was a place that she was unwilling to go. He couldn't have her. She deserved so much better in a man. In a relationship. In the great love of her life and father of her children. Not someone who was so repugnant and obsessed with molding her into someone she wasn't. She would rather die than succumb to his unreasonable demands. No matter what personal sacrifices she would have to make.

Sucking in a deep breath, Giselle ran up the quarter-turn staircase in the waterfront mansion to the second story, the determined attacker in hot pursuit. If she could just get to the primary suite and lock the door behind her, maybe she could survive the ordeal by calling the police to come to her rescue. Only then could she ever hope to have a normal life, with a normal man to give her love to.

She raced in her bare feet across the hardwood flooring in the long hallway, nearly tripping but correcting herself from tumbling. But even losing half a step shortened the distance between her and the man who wanted her dead. Still, she forged ahead, reaching the room she'd once shared with her hunter, but seeing it now as nothing more than a prison.

Inside, she barely had a chance to take in the expensive Italian furnishings while simultaneously attempting to slam the door shut before he could stop her, when he was able to do just that.

Using his greater strength, he forced the door open, knocking her to the floor in the process. Scrambling to her feet, she ran toward the king-size bed, hoping to somehow get to the other side and maybe onto the balcony. Instead, he caught up to her, grabbed her by the hair and threw her down hard onto the dark blue comforter.

Before she could even breathe, he had climbed on top of her, where he placed large hands around her neck, his face contorted with anger like a man possessed. She tried to fight him off but to no avail, as she felt her strength fading—along with her very life.

He was strangling her to death. And there was nothing she could do about it. Other than accept her fate.

She looked into the evil eyes of death. Glaring back at her was Justin.

Giselle tried to scratch his face, but he stayed just out of reach of her flailing hands and fingernails. Before she could breathe her last breath, she managed to squeeze from her mouth that she hated him with a passion—to which he seemed to draw upon in his contorted face and sick satisfaction in achieving his ultimate objective of taking her life.

THE SCREAM THAT threatened to shatter her eardrums was, in fact, coming from Giselle's own vocal cords as she opened her eyes. It took her a moment to adjust to the darkness and surroundings to recognize that she was in the small bedroom of her Taller's Creek apartment, lying atop a cotton quilt on her sleigh bed in the wee hours of the morning.

It was only a dream, Giselle told herself, sitting up and catching her breath, feeling relieved. She still needed a moment to regain her equilibrium. Even then, she half expected Justin to emerge from the shadows and finish off what he had started in her nightmare. She froze in that instant—darting her eyes this way and that—before deciding that he wasn't there.

But Muffin was. Apparently having heard her cries of dreaming anguish, the kitten had wakened from sleeping comfortably in her kitten bed in the corner and jumped up on the bed out of concern for her and was cuddled against her.

"I'm fine, Muffin," Giselle uttered appreciatively, holding the kitten to her chest. "It was just a silly nightmare." In truth, she didn't consider it silly at all but rather a manifestation of a nightmare ex-fiancé that she hadn't been able to entirely shake, in spite of her best efforts to the contrary. The latest episode had been undoubtedly triggered by the untimely deaths of two people she'd been acquainted with—in addition to imagined sightings of Justin in Taller's Creek.

Giselle cringed while running her hand gently along Muffin's back. She regretted not having come clean with Quincy right from the start on the man she had escaped from, bringing her to Alaska. But she'd been wary of trusting anyone too soon about her past. Even a person who was employed by the Alaska Bureau of Investigation.

Now she realized that some chances were worth taking in life and that it was okay to trust her instincts. Particularly where Quincy was concerned. She could only hope he didn't hold this against her and pull back from any chance that they might be able to establish a relationship in her post-Justin life.

If only she could be certain, once and for all, that he was, in fact, out of her life for good. Perhaps Quincy would be able to give her that reassurance.

Until then, Giselle was resolved to not allow herself to be spooked by the specter of Justin. No matter how hard he had made this for her—even from a distance. Assuming that was indeed the case.

She got up in her short pajamas and, along with Muffin, went into the kitchen. Turning on the light, Giselle adjusted her eyes accordingly, refusing to think that Justin was lurking somewhere in the apartment. Waiting to attack her. As it was, there was no sign that her personal space had been breached.

She opened the refrigerator and grabbed a bottle of water for her and kitten liquid for Muffin.

After they drank, with Muffin deciding to curl up on an upholstered lounge chair, Giselle went back to bed. She imagined Quincy being beside her, cuddling, while fearing that falling asleep would result in a repeat performance of Justin trying to strangle her to death.

Instead, there was no nightmare this time around. Giselle slept peacefully, making the most of the hours she had left before starting a new day in earnest.

Chapter Seven

Sergeant Miriam Fontaine sat on a metal chair in an interview room at the Taller's Creek Police Department on Lamotte Street. On the other side of the wooden table, Armand Younis was seated. The forty-one-year-old construction worker and former boyfriend of Yuki Kotake had come in voluntarily to, as he'd put it, clear the air as it related to the fashion designer's death.

With the investigation still underway, Miriam was interested in what he had to say after the body had been discovered the day before. She regarded the beefy ex, who had a blond mane in a combed-backward style and wore square glasses over blue eyes. "Thanks for coming in," she told him, saving her the trouble of looking for him, should it have proven necessary down the line. "Sorry about Ms. Kotake… If you have any information on what happened to her, I'm happy to take your statement."

Armand nodded and said, "They say that Yuki killed herself." He grimaced. "She'd never do that," he argued.

Miriam had heard it all before. It was always easier to be in denial in these situations, even when the evidence suggested otherwise. She was guilty of this herself from time to time when tragedy hit too close to home. In this instance, Ballistics had linked the shell casing recovered at the scene and bullet removed from the victim to the Walther PDP near the body. Unless, of course, there was a strong reason for the ex-boyfriend to believe someone else could have wanted her dead.

Without giving away anything that might compromise the investigation, Miriam noted, "The firearm found near Ms. Kotake's body was legally purchased by her. Also, according to the victim's sister, Willow Kotake, she was suicidal."

"Yuki would not have committed suicide," Armand maintained, narrowing his eyes. "She loved life too much for that. Her antidepressants were working. No, someone else had to have been there…"

"There was no sign of forced entry," Miriam said, while conceding that the fashion designer could have let her killer in unsuspectingly. At least in theory. Including her ex. Was he trying to confess in a roundabout way? "Where were you when this happened?" she asked, providing him with an estimated time of death.

Without prelude, he replied confidently, "I was in Seattle, working on a project. There are plenty of people to vouch for that. I just got back this morning after hearing the news about Yuki."

Recognizing that this was easy enough to confirm, Miriam had no reason to detain him. But she would keep an open mind on the circumstances of Yuki Kotake's death till the results came in on the autopsy and gunshot residue.

THAT AFTERNOON, Quincy sat at his desk, comparing findings from the State Medical Examiner's Office and the

ABI Scientific Crime Detection Laboratory regarding the death of Yuki Kotake.

According to the autopsy report, the victim had died from a gunshot to the right side of her head, causing serious damage to both her brain and skull. The manner of death had been ruled to be likely self-inflicted. With a history of using antidepressants, a forensic toxicology test was still pending but unlikely to change the basic premise on the conclusion of how she'd died.

Quincy zeroed in on the gun-residue aspect of the autopsy report. It was unclear just how much had been found on one of Yuki Kotake's hands. The GSR kit was sent to the crime lab for further analysis. Staring at their report, he saw that it indicated that particles were present on the dead woman's right hand that were indicative of gunshot primer residue. Or, in other words, the forensic evidence suggested that the victim had been holding the pistol she'd owned when one slug had gone into her head.

Looks like it was, in fact, suicide, Quincy told himself, trusting the joint evidence to that effect. This certainly seemed to throw cold water on the notion that Giselle's former fiancé had somehow engineered it to make Yuki Kotake's death appear to be self-inflicted. That said, Quincy admitted that stranger things had happened over the years in his line of work. Could this be one of them, against the odds? Would the same be true of Neve Chenoweth's accidental death as well?

After bringing Lieutenant Valdez up to speed on Yuki Kotake's tragic ending, Quincy got on the computer to do some digging on Justin Buckner. First and foremost, he wanted to see if the man had committed any crimes—especially serious offenses. Accessing the National Crime Information Center, Quincy ran a criminal history check on Buckner. He quickly discovered that Giselle's former fiancé did have a rap sheet—including arrests for assault, drug possession, fraud and threatening a police officer. None of these had resulted in conviction, as the charges had either been dropped or otherwise disappeared.

Someone must have had his back, Quincy couldn't help but think, suspicious. Just what else might he have done and gotten away with—could he be making Giselle's life a living hell when they were together, by making real or implied threats toward her physical safety, health and well-being?

Gazing at Buckner's mug shot, Quincy imagined Giselle being involved with him. He quickly dismissed the unappealing thought, rejecting the notion of competing with the man for her affections when it was obvious that Giselle wanted nothing more to do with Buckner, given the extreme measures she'd taken to get away from him.

Quincy got on the phone with the Federal Bureau of Investigation. Or, more specifically, Daniel Malaterre, a fellow Eyak member and buddy since grade school. He'd joined the Bureau nearly a decade ago and was currently the special agent in charge at the field office in Omaha, Nebraska, where Daniel lived with his wife and college sweetheart, Shania, and their newborn daughter, Connie.

Daniel answered the video call on the second ring. His narrow face appeared on the cell phone screen, along with black hair in a textured cut and brown eyes. Sporting a crooked grin, he said, "Hey, Trooper."

"Hey." Quincy grinned, remembering their days growing up. Without preface, he asked him, "Got a sec?"

"Yeah, I have a few minutes to spare." Daniel sounded like he was adjusting in his office desk chair. "What's up?"

"I need some info on a guy," Quincy told him. "Name's Justin Buckner. Lives in Chesapeake, Virginia."

"Looking for anything specific?"

"I need to know if Buckner may have taken a plane to Alaska in the last month." Quincy stood up. "Or even to the state of Washington or Canada," he added, realizing that Buckner could have driven to Alaska from one of those places, theoretically.

"What has he done?" Daniel asked curiously.

"Probably nothing in this state," Quincy admitted honestly. "It's more of a personal request, on behalf of someone who used to be engaged to Buckner and wants to be reasonably certain that he's not stalking her."

"Okay. Let's see what I can find out…"

Quincy was put on hold and waited for him to use his FBI connections to access passenger info from a travel database on bookings worldwide. It operated in real time to help the Bureau track suspects, or potential suspects, and their movements on airlines, from reservations to seat assignments and more. If Buckner had boarded a plane under his own name anytime recently, it would show up.

After a few minutes, Daniel came back on the line and said, "There's no indication that Justin Buckner has flown to Alaska, Washington, Oregon, California or Canada in the past month. Or, for that matter, anywhere else…" He took a breath. "Of course, if Buckner was traveling under an assumed name, then it might be a different story."

"All right." Quincy had no reason to believe that was the case for the time being. The more likely scenario was that Buckner was not in Taller's Creek right now, stalking Giselle, much less involved in the deaths of Yuki Kotake or Neve Chenoweth. "Thanks for checking."

"No problem. Actually, I've come up with something else on Buckner that may interest you…"

"I'm listening," Quincy said.

"He's currently being investigated by the feds—including the Securities and Exchange Commission—for wire fraud and embezzlement in relation to Buckner's business as a certified financial planner in Chesapeake."

"Hmm…" Quincy was thinking out loud. "So Buckner is in trouble?"

"I'd say so," Daniel told him. "From what I'm seeing, I'd say that an arrest is imminent."

And, in the process, likely to keep him preoccupied with trying to stay out of prison, Quincy told himself. "I'll be sure to pass that on to Giselle," he said, knowing that would ease her fears regarding Buckner.

"One other thing I've come across in the investigation…" Daniel mentioned. "Four years ago, Buckner was questioned about the disappearance of a waitress named Jenna Sweeney. But apparently nothing became of this, and it didn't go any further."

"I see," Quincy mused, wondering if Giselle knew about this Jenna Sweeney. Or if Buckner could still be a threat to Giselle, should she ever set foot outside of Alaska.

After catching up for a few minutes, Quincy disconnected from Daniel and headed out to share the latest news with Giselle.

While on his way to the park where they'd agreed to meet, Quincy got a call from his sister, Olivia. He sensed it pertained to his nephew's birthday party, which included Quincy's parents driving up from Juneau, feeling that the more than twenty-hour trip by car was well worth it.

Putting his cell phone on speaker, Quincy said in an affable tone of voice, "Hey, sis."

"Hi, Quincy." Olivia waited a beat, then said, "I know you're pretty busy, but just thought I'd remind you that Todd's birthday bash is Saturday. Hope you can make it." She added as further incentive, "Everyone will be there."

"I wouldn't miss it," Quincy told her, smiling, even if he had missed his niece Krista's birthday party last year, as duty had called.

"Wonderful." Olivia's voice rose excitedly.

"Can't wait to see Mom and Dad," he told her, wishing there was more time to visit them in Juneau.

"They will be just as happy to see you!"

Quincy watched the road ahead of him thoughtfully. "Do you mind if I bring a guest?"

"Of course not," Olivia assured him.

"Good."

"Who's the guest…?"

"Her name's Giselle," he answered. "She works at the bookstore where I picked up some books for Todd—and got a few for Krista too while I was at it."

"How nice."

Olivia was silent for a moment, and Quincy could read her mind in wondering about Giselle, knowing that he didn't make a habit of inviting anyone to meet his family. But this time it felt right, wanting to make Giselle feel even more at home in Alaska. "I think she'd like meeting everyone," he said intuitively.

Olivia asked, "New woman in your life...?"

Quincy pondered the notion. "One can always hope," he answered candidly, realizing that they weren't quite there yet to define this as a relationship based on one kiss, satisfying as it had been.

"Yes, one can." His sister laughed understandingly. "Giselle's always welcome at our house. You, too."

Quincy grinned, taking the hint about wanting him to visit more often. Now maybe he had a good excuse to do just that, if Giselle planned to stick around and accompany him. Or would she be more likely to bolt from Alaska once her ex-fiancé had been arrested and was no longer an impediment to her life in Virginia?

GISELLE SPOTTED QUINCY at Teary Lake Park on Dakley Road. He waved to her while standing on the shore by the lake. She walked past some aspen trees toward him and wondered if he had frightening news that Justin had indeed located her and, in the process, was making his presence felt by going after people she knew.

I have to stay positive and assume that isn't the case, Giselle told herself, wanting to believe that Neve's and Yuki's unfortunate deaths were unrelated to her ex-fiancé, just as Quincy had intimated from his investigations.

"Hey." He eyed her with a handsome smile.

"Hi." She held his gaze guardedly and got right to it, asking, "What did you learn about Justin...?"

Quincy touched the brim of his campaign hat and said coolly, "Well, the good news is that as near as my FBI contact was able to determine, there's no evidence that

Buckner has traveled by plane to anywhere in Alaska, much less in the vicinity of Taller's Creek in the last month or so. Same is true for the West Coast or Canada. At least using his real name. Odds are that your ex has not been stalking you or played any role in the deaths of Neve Chenoweth or Yuki Kotake—whose death was ruled by the medical examiner to be a probable suicide, when combined with her history of depression and suicidal ideation. As if that isn't enough proof," he said firmly, "gun residue found on Yuki's hand strongly suggested that she was holding the firearm that was used to kill her."

"I'm glad to hear that Justin wasn't responsible for their deaths," Giselle admitted as she glanced out at the lake and back while feeling relieved on that front, in spite of still grieving the untimely demise of her friends. "And that he isn't in Taller's Creek as a stalker—intent on intimidating me for his own sick pleasure."

"It certainly doesn't appear to be a real cause for concern," Quincy stressed again, a catch to his voice.

Giselle picked up on this as well as his emphasis on the *good news* about Justin, as though there was bad news to follow. "What else did you learn?" She hesitated to ask but sensed there was a real need to know.

He drew a breath and answered straightforwardly, "Buckner is under federal investigation for embezzlement and wire fraud regarding his work as a financial planner."

Giselle cocked a brow. "Oh, really?"

"Yeah." Quincy jutted his chin. "It appears as though Buckner has been filling his pockets, perhaps for years, at the expense of those entrusting him with their funds."

"This isn't really news to me," she said candidly.

"After I'd been in Taller's Creek for about six months, curiosity—and perhaps instincts—made me do a little research online for news out of Chesapeake related to Justin. I saw that he was being investigated by the federal government for the crimes you've described. Then it seemed like the investigation had run out of steam and that Justin may have been let off the hook."

"Not by a long shot," Quincy asserted squarely. "It often takes time—in some cases, years—before the feds can build a solid enough case to put the hammer down on a suspect. That seems to be the case here, with Buckner living on borrowed time…"

Giselle took a breath. "In truth, I've always been suspicious that Justin could be stealing clients' money. Or otherwise enriching himself illegally. But I had no proof to support this feeling." Her nose wrinkled guiltily. "If only I had. It could've saved his clients from losing their money, perhaps forever, that they invested with him."

"None of what Buckner is being accused of and investigated for is your fault, Giselle," Quincy insisted, setting his jaw. "In any event, I'm told that he could be arrested soon, which would likely keep Justin Buckner out of your life—and his bilked clients—for years to come."

"Good." Giselle grinned, feeling as if she might finally be able to let her guard down in a way that had been impossible as long as Justin was free to pursue her to the ends of the earth. "Honestly, I never want to see that man again!"

"You don't have to." Quincy fixed her with a straight gaze contemplatively. "There's something else that's worth mentioning regarding Buckner—"

Do I want to know? Giselle mused, ill at ease, but uttered, "What is it?"

"Four years ago, he was questioned by the police about the disappearance of a waitress," Quincy revealed. "Apparently there wasn't enough evidence to charge him with anything, so it ended there. No word on what happened to the woman—if anything at all…"

"Hope she's all right." Giselle's voice shook with obvious concern. Knowing Justin as she did, she wouldn't put anything past him. Including being obsessed with someone else before they met. And exacting revenge upon her if the woman wanted out of the relationship. Had that occurred here? *Or am I allowing my imagination to create a crime by my ex that never happened?* she asked herself.

"Me too," Quincy told her and added, "I'm sure if there was any evidence of wrongdoing by Buckner, the authorities would have kept him on their radar."

Giselle nodded, as this made sense to her. She forced herself to block out a persistent feeling that the news of Justin being a suspect in a woman's disappearance was a forerunner to his fixation on her and how he'd vowed to never let go of her.

She lifted her eyes to Quincy and asked, "Would you like to come for dinner tonight?"

He met her gaze. "I have a better idea. How about I invite you to dinner at my place—if you're comfortable with that?"

"I am," she responded quickly, with a reassuring smile on her face. "I'd love to have dinner at your house."

"Good. Then it's a date." He grinned back at her. "I'll text you my address."

"Okay." Giselle looked forward to them spending more personal time together and also saw it as a way to further push Justin out of her mind, once and for all. With a much better man to give her attention to.

JUSTIN HID BEHIND a large spruce tree, watching surreptitiously as Giselle talked to a state trooper in the park. He was guessing it was about him. Ironically, even if he were to reveal himself to them, Justin wasn't sure that his ex-fiancée would recognize the man she'd promised herself to.

After allowing her to catch a glimpse of him at the bookstore window and in the wine and liquor section of the grocery store, making sure the image was one that was pretty close to how he'd looked when they'd last spoken three years ago, Justin had taken steps to give himself a makeover. Gone were the golden locks covering his head, replaced with baldness that was shaven specifically to alter his appearance. And instead of being smooth shaven, as had been the preference for much of his adult life, he had deliberately gone with a five o'clock shadow to camouflage his facial features.

Similarly, he had changed his style of clothing to both fit into his new environment and throw off Giselle. His fashionable designer suits and Oxford shoes had been replaced with camp shirts, jeans and chukka boots or sneakers, depending on what he was doing.

At the moment, he was wearing black sneakers, as Justin regarded Giselle and the trooper, while keeping himself out of their line of vision. He couldn't hear what they were saying, but the fact that Giselle was meeting with a law enforcement officer told Justin all he needed to know. Did his ex-fiancée believe she was safe from him if she reported her suspicions to the authorities? *If so, think again...* he thought.

Or was there more to this get-together by the lake?

Justin mused, pinching the bridge of his nose. As it was, he'd taken extraordinary steps to stay one step—maybe two or three steps—ahead of the law. He knew that he was under investigation by the feds. And that he was guilty of wrongdoing, but it was too much to pass up on when the opportunities presented themselves as clear as day.

When his lawyer had informed him three weeks ago that an arrest was all but imminent and that he might want to start to get his affairs in order, Justin hadn't hesitated to formulate a plan to escape. He had no desire to spend the rest of his life in prison. Especially now that he had discovered Giselle's whereabouts and wanted retribution for humiliating him and stomping on his love for her like it was worthless.

He'd emptied his bank accounts, to the degree he could, and fled Chesapeake—only telling his parents that he'd needed to get away for a while to clear his head. He didn't want them involved in his legal troubles any more than necessary.

Knowing he couldn't travel safely and freely under his own name, Justin had stolen the name of a recently deceased client, Jesse Teague, using his new identity to make his way to Alaska.

To Giselle's hideaway.

As soon as he dealt with her, so that Giselle could never again flee to what she mistakenly believed was a safe haven, Justin planned to leave the country altogether. He would settle in a place where there was no extradition treaty with the US, such as Taiwan, Cuba or Morocco. Or maybe even Vietnam.

But not just yet.

Not when there was still work—and some play—to be done under the moniker Jesse Teague.

Justin chuckled wickedly under his breath. He continued to give Giselle and the trooper the benefit of his attention for a while longer before quietly slipping away.

Chapter Eight

Quincy had admittedly not spent as much time in the kitchen as he would have liked. At least not as a cook, having settled more often than not these days for microwave dishes and takeout. But then again, there hadn't been much of a reason to put his cooking skills to the test. Till now.

Having learned some great authentic dishes from his mother and both grandmothers, it was time he made good use of that. Giselle would give him that opportunity. Not to mention it was another chance to further their involvement with one another. He was glad she was amenable to it.

That said, Quincy was a little worried that with things apparently coming to a head with Justin Buckner's impending arrest, it might result in Giselle leaving Alaska and returning to Virginia once the dust settled. If so, where would that leave them and what Quincy had hoped might be the match made in heaven that he had longed to find with someone?

He tried not to think about it too much as he stood in the kitchen preparing the meal, which included moose steak, fondant potatoes, sweet carrots, fry bread, salmonberries and Alaskan ice cream for dessert. They would wash the meal down with red wine.

Quincy glanced down at his light blue button-up shirt and dark trousers worn with loafers before laying out dishes, glasses and silverware on the rustic red-cedar dining room table and heading back to the kitchen for final preparations. He wanted this to be a worthwhile meal and enjoyable experience for Giselle.

When she arrived like clockwork, he couldn't help but be thoroughly captivated by her. Even at a glance, Giselle was the picture of beauty, a sight for sore eyes or any other adage Quincy could think of while dressed in a yellow flutter-sleeve top, white linen pants and ankle-strap sandals. He picked up a faint citrusy scent she wore that was appealing to him.

"Hey," he said smoothly, offering a sheepish grin.

"Hey." She showed her pretty teeth.

"Come in." After she did so, Quincy greeted Giselle with a gentlemanly kiss on the cheek, as if they had never kissed on the lips before. He hoped they might pick up where they'd left off in that regard later. "Here we are…"

Gazing about the downstairs, Giselle marveled, "Nice place you have."

Downplaying it, Quincy responded honestly, "I think it's way too big for just one person."

"And whose fault is that?" she teased him, batting her lashes.

"Point taken. I'll have to work on that." He laughed. "Hope you've worked up a good appetite?"

"Starved, actually," she indicated and then sniffed. "It smells amazing."

"Should taste even better," he promised. "Coming right up. Make yourself at home."

"Okay."

Apparently that meant helping him in the kitchen and seeming as natural with it as though they were living together. The notion was something that agreed with Quincy as they sat down in rustic dining chairs kitty-corner from one another.

Giselle wasted no time in saying ardently, after tasting the moose steak, fry bread and fondant potatoes, "I love it!"

Quincy grinned, forking a carrot. "You can thank my grandma Jeanne, as this is one of her favorite meals."

"I'd be happy to." Giselle nibbled on the fry bread. "Just point me in the right direction."

"Unfortunately she passed away a few years ago," he hated to say. "But she'll always be around in spirit—and I'm certain Grandma Jeanne would've been thrilled that you're enjoying the food."

"It's hard not to," Giselle maintained while trying out the salmonberries.

Quincy sliced into his own moose steak and said, "I'm glad you like it."

Later, they had Alaskan ice cream and coffee.

"This is really good," she told him gleefully, running her tongue across her mouth.

He chuckled with amusement. "Yeah, I can see you're enjoying it."

Giselle colored. "I don't mean to make a pig out of myself."

"A pig you could never be—not even on your worst day," Quincy assured her and got a laugh out of her. After a moment or two of enjoying each other's company, he decided to bring up something that had been weighing on his mind. "So, is he why you gave up dancing when you moved to Taller's Creek?" It didn't take much to speculate that she wanted to keep a low profile—in case he used that to track her down.

As if reading his mind, she sipped her coffee and answered musingly, "Yes, as a matter of fact. I figured that if I opened up a dance studio anywhere else, Justin would surely find a way to learn about it and come after me. I couldn't afford to take the chance of that happening, so I simply had to find another way to make a living."

Quincy tasted his own coffee, frowning. "Sorry that Buckner put you in such a position where you were forced to turn away from something you loved."

"Me too." She made a face. "As much as I hate him for it, though, I have to take some responsibility for the decisions I've made—which includes being too naive at the time to see what a big mistake I was making in ever getting involved with the likes of Justin."

"We're all entitled to make a few mistakes in our lives," Quincy told her, reaching his hand out to her. "I've certainly made my fair share and have learned from them, making me a better person."

"Something tells me that you've always been a better person," Giselle said flatly, a soft smile on her face. "Especially compared to the man I wish I'd never met."

"I'd like to think so," Quincy admitted. Still, he was flattered to be thought of in such a way and more than happy to command her attention as she commanded his.

"I'd love to check out the rest of your house," she told him.

"Of course." He grinned at her, wishing he had given her the grand tour sooner. "Why don't I show you around…"

They both stood after finishing off their coffees.

AFTER LEADING THE WAY up the open riser staircase to the second story, Giselle ventured off on her own, taking in the various well-appointed rooms with their rustic furniture and picture windows, while Quincy stood in the hall patiently. When she scooted past him somewhat nervously and got to the primary bedroom with an en suite, Giselle stepped inside and took a look around. She wasn't at all disappointed as her gaze fell on the king-size wood bed, covered with a gray-and-red striped comforter.

Feeling Quincy come up behind her and breathe on her neck, Giselle felt turned on as she faced him.

"Well, what do you think?" he asked, holding her gaze.

"Do you really want to know?" Her tone was daring.

He smiled playfully. "Yeah, let me have it."

"Okay, if you insist." Giselle gathered up her nerve to match her suddenly overwhelming needs. She cupped Quincy's chiseled cheeks and planted a kiss on his hard mouth, savoring the taste of him. This made her even more desirous. She made herself unlock their lips and uttered anxiously, "What I think is… I want you to make love to me."

Quincy gave her a straight look and asked in earnest, "Are you sure that you're ready for this?"

Giselle touched her tingling lips. "If you want to know the truth, I've been ready." She wondered if he had been of the same mind but had merely been waiting for the right moment to arrive.

"So have I," he told her deeply. "I want you, too, Giselle. Badly."

The notion thrilled her. "Do you have protection?" she thought to ask, knowing that being responsible was important for both of them.

"I do." Quincy smiled. "Wait here."

"Oh, I'm not going anywhere," she promised.

Giselle watched as he went into the en suite bathroom and returned with a foil wrapper, tossing it onto the bed. It was all she needed as she began to remove her clothes, and he did the same. Exposing herself like this was unnerving, to say the least. What if he didn't like what he saw? She had always prided herself on staying in shape and was proportionate from head to toe with medium-sized firm breasts. But some men preferred more of this or less of that. Would she measure up for him?

As if he were reading into her thoughts, Quincy gave her a once-over and said boldly, "You're stunning...everywhere!"

Giselle smiled, feeling reassured with the praise, and eyed his taut nakedness and six-pack abs. "I can honestly say the same thing about you," she confessed, her libido rising like the tide with each passing second that they were not in his bed.

Clearly on the same wavelength, Quincy scooped her up into his powerful arms and carried her to the bed, setting her down gently before climbing in beside her.

What happened next was as much a blur to Giselle as it was satisfying beyond anything she could imagine. They kissed passionately like there was no more tomorrow and engaged in foreplay that had her body on fire all over and within. She could tell that the same was true for him.

When she could stand it no more, Giselle demanded, "Take me—now!"

"With pleasure…and then some," Quincy told her on a breath.

He ripped open the packet and slid on the condom before making his way between her splayed legs, atop her, where Giselle was more than welcoming, as ready for this as her deepest fantasies for the trooper. She came almost instantly as he plunged deep inside of her.

But even with that sheer joy, Giselle knew that the experience could only be complete and fulfilling when they rose to the heights of carnal pleasure together. As such, she kissed him and moved her body in a way to encourage his own climax, which had him shuddering with its powerful release.

With a sharp gasp from his thrusts, she brought their bodies together, and Giselle had a second, even stronger orgasm and, with Quincy, rode the wave of sexual ecstasy together.

When it was over and he rolled off her, each catching their breaths, Giselle blushed and still had to admit unabashedly, "Wow! That was amazing!"

"You're telling me." Quincy laughed. "It was well worth the wait—trust me. But it's *you* that's truly amazing," he uttered, sighing.

Her lashes fluttered. "Oh, you think so?"

"I know so." He kissed her moist shoulder. "Thanks for coming into my life."

She smiled. "Actually, I think it was the other way around, if I recall correctly."

Quincy waited a beat before propping up on an elbow

and saying, "So, do you plan to stick around here a while now that Buckner's about to be arrested?"

Giselle paused contemplatively for a long moment, then admitted, "I hadn't really thought about it. I only knew that as long as Justin was still operating freely in Chesapeake, I could never go back there."

"And now?"

She understood that he was trying to gauge whether or not what had just happened between them was something they could build upon. Or if it was just a flash in the pan with no legs for long-term possibilities.

Had she ever planned to return home? Or had she assumed that Justin would make that impossible, without really thinking beyond that?

But that was before you entered my life, Giselle told herself, regarding Quincy. He gave her a reason to want to stay, over and beyond having made a home for herself in Alaska the last year and a half.

"I'd like to remain here and see how things go," she told him honestly, knowing there was nothing truly awaiting her back in Virginia.

Quincy grinned, looking relieved. "Good."

Though she felt the same way, Giselle couldn't help but turn the tables on him, to see his reaction. "Do you think you would ever be willing to move from Alaska yourself?" Or were his roots there so solid that the thought of ever relocating was a nonstarter? Even if it involved matters of the heart.

Quincy stared at the question for an agonizing few seconds, after which he looked her right in the eye and answered, "I've spent my whole life living in this great state and just assumed I'd be here forever. But truthfully, with a line of work that's in demand across the country, I'd move elsewhere in a heartbeat if I had a good enough reason—" his gaze sharpened on her "—such as that special someone who made the end more than justify the means."

She beamed. "Good answer."

"Just calling the balls and strikes as I see them," he claimed.

"Hmm…" Giselle took that for what it was worth. In this instance, they definitely seemed to be on the same team insofar as being open to whatever could come their way in seeing each other. She leaned into him and kissed him, a fresh round of desire rippling through her. "Care to go a second round?" she challenged him.

He kissed her back heartily and said through her open mouth willingly, "Absolutely. Let's do this…"

QUINCY TOOK HIS TIME making love to Giselle the second time around, going the extra mile in pleasuring her in every way she expressed through her words, gasps, touches and reaction to his actions. He wanted the experience to be one that demonstrated just how good they were together. While he'd been concerned that she might bolt once Justin Buckner was in custody, these fears had apparently been unwarranted as Giselle seemed just as anxious to see where things could go between them as Quincy was. He sure as hell would not run away from a woman who checked all the boxes for him. That included being as incredible in the nude as he had fantasized about, and much more. Hopefully he could fit the bill for what she deserved in a man for an intimate relationship.

Once he knew Giselle had been thoroughly satisfied, based on her deep sighs, murmurs, urging him on and tenseness of her body before it relaxed, Quincy had no need to hold back as he let loose in reaching his own climax, enhanced by her own cries of sexual bliss. Together, they peaked at just the right time and took a few moments afterward to recover their equilibrium.

As they cuddled in his bed, Quincy remembered he had been meaning to ask Giselle something. Now was as good a time as any. "How do you feel about going to my nephew's birthday party on Saturday?" he asked, hoping she wouldn't pass on the opportunity to meet his family. "My parents will be there."

"I'd love to come," Giselle said easily, then added tentatively, "if you're sure that's what you want...?"

"I'm sure," Quincy reiterated. "It'll be fun." Not to mention it would give everyone a chance to see and talk to someone he wanted in his life.

She smiled. "Then I'm in."

"Cool." He kissed her, as if to seal the deal.

Chapter Nine

On Saturday, Giselle sat in silence in the passenger seat of Quincy's Subaru Forester as he drove to the home of his sister, Olivia, and her husband, Kenneth Wheeler, in Nikiski, just off the Kenai Spur Highway. Admittedly, Giselle was a bit nervous about meeting the family of the man she had made love to last night. In the process, he had managed to win her over in more ways than one. Or in ways that counted most in what she looked for in a partner.

Not only had Quincy proven to be as gentle in bed as he was totally attentive to her needs, but he'd succeeded in making her heart skip some beats and more. It made her eager to see how far this could go between them. Right down to considering remaining in Taller's Creek for the foreseeable future—even when Justin's arrest would give her the freedom to return to Chesapeake and pick up her life where she'd left off.

But exactly what type of life would I be heading back to? Giselle asked herself as she glanced at Quincy, who seemed to be caught up in his own thoughts as he turned onto Lighthouse Avenue. One where memories of Justin's control over her and his neurotic behavior would only haunt her? Did she really want to turn her back on the potential a relationship with Quincy offered in Alaska for an unknown future in Virginia?

The answer was no. A definitive no. She needed to see this through with the gorgeous trooper beside her and not run away from what could well become her destiny. And his, for that matter.

This included doing her best to make a good impression on those whom Quincy held dear.

He swung a left on Rozella Drive and, seconds later, pulled up to a three-level house, bordered by mature pine and spruce trees. In the driveway, there were several late-model vehicles.

"Well, here we are." Quincy broke the silence, flashing her a grin out of the corner of his mouth.

Giselle regarded him cautiously. "Are you sure it's a good thing that I meet your family right now...?"

"I'm positive," he insisted. "Trust me, they won't need any help from me to be sold on just how wonderful you are, Giselle!"

She blushed. "If you say so."

Not that she was opposed to taking this next step with him, as Giselle—with her own parents out of the picture and no siblings—wanted to feel that familial sense of belonging that she'd never felt with Justin's parents, who were as cold and distant as he was domineering and needy. They'd made it clear to her that they'd thought Justin could do better in a girlfriend, much less a fiancée. But he'd seemed to have a mind of his own in opposing them.

I only wish Justin had taken their advice and turned his attention elsewhere, Giselle told herself. It would have saved them both the trouble of being in a relationship doomed to failure. Better late than never.

On the other hand, she was trusting Quincy that his family would be more welcoming and one she could become connected to as she was starting to connect with the trooper himself.

QUINCY WAS MORE THAN HAPPY to introduce Giselle to his parents, sister, brother-in-law, niece and nephew. As expected, they all warmed up to her instantly, seeing in Giselle what he did—a woman who was not only beautiful but had a good heart and soul and cared about people. That was pretty much all he could ask for in a person Quincy wanted in his life.

But he got even more when Giselle commanded the attention of Todd, his now five-year-old nephew and his six-year-old sister, Krista. They were wide eyed and all ears as Giselle read from some of the books Quincy had bought for them and seemed as natural in so doing as if they were her own kids. This gave him a real sense of just what a great mother she would make whenever Giselle decided to have children of her own.

If I'm lucky, maybe I'll be the father of those children—however many it ends up being, Quincy told himself wistfully in the large, carpeted family room with rattan furnishings, where everyone had gathered. He noted Giselle talking with his parents, both in their early sixties and in good health, while sitting on the wicker sofa. His sister, Olivia, joined in on the conversation as her kids were playing with toys on the floor.

Quincy took a sip from the bottle of beer he was holding as he stood beside his brother-in-law, Kenneth. The thirty-three-year-old petroleum engineer was a member of the Yakutat Tlingit Tribe and six feet, six inches tall with dark long hair parted in the middle.

"Where have you been hiding her?" Kenneth asked, drinking beer.

Quincy laughed. "She's always been in plain view. I just needed the right time to bring Giselle around."

"Glad you did. Looks like she's fitting right in."

"That was the plan," Quincy admitted, marveling at just how comfortable Giselle seemed around everyone. And vice versa. He saw this as a good sign that they really could make a go of this, with family an important part of his life and culture. He only wished her own parents were still alive for him to get to know.

"How did you manage to hit it off?" Kenneth asked curiously.

"It wasn't that difficult," he told him candidly. "Just came naturally." He added for context that they had met under less-than-ideal circumstances, when needing to question Giselle about the death of Neve Chenoweth. That notwithstanding, they'd still been able to find common ground, a mutual attraction, and go from there.

"She seems like a keeper to me," his brother-in-law said flatly.

"Me too," Olivia pitched in, walking up to them. "She's wonderful!"

Quincy gazed at his twenty-nine-year-old sister, a stay-at-home mom who was much shorter than her husband but taller than most women and slender, with long and wavy cappuccino-colored hair and brown eyes. "Tell me something I don't know," he teased her.

"How about that Giselle would love to have a boy

and girl of her own someday?" Olivia told him. "At the very least," she added.

"Really?" Though surprised by the specifics, Quincy was already certain that Giselle had the maternal instincts necessary to be a great mother.

"Guess she would have gotten around to mentioning this to you the closer you become, big brother." Olivia smiled at him. "Since Mom and Dad want more grandchildren to dote over while they're still alive, this would certainly work for them—as long as you're the father. I'm just saying…"

"So you are." Quincy chuckled, while feeling the pressure of measuring up to his sister and her kids in their parents' eyes. He felt more than up to the challenge if things continued to progress with Giselle.

When he looked at Kenneth for support, his brother-in-law laughed and said, "This is a hole you'll have to dig yourself out of, one way or the other."

"Duly noted." Quincy laughed and gave him a friendly pat on the shoulder before making his way over to Giselle and his parents while hoping they weren't going overboard in giving her the third degree. Or could it be the other way around?

ON SUNDAY, Giselle went jogging down the sidewalk, with quick sprints on the street itself when there was no traffic. She kept an eye out for moose or other wildlife that might literally happen to cross her path here or there.

She thought about visiting with Quincy's family the day before and how nice everyone had been to her. It was definitely a pleasant feeling to be welcomed by those who could somehow become her own extended family.

She was certainly open to the possibility, wanting nothing more than to find love and give love to someone worthy of this. Quincy seemed like he could be that person.

He sure does know how to make me feel special, Giselle told herself, realizing just how much she needed that. She'd wondered for so long if it was even possible to get involved with someone again, with the lingering thoughts of Justin a living nightmare still not far from the surface. But with Quincy, it was so much different. He got her in the most meaningful way. Just as she got him. It seemed like they could really be onto something here.

Only time would tell. And patience, both ways.

As she continued to jog, happy for the exercise and wanting more than ever to stay in shape now that there was someone in her life to keep pace with in that regard, Giselle could hear what sounded like hurried footsteps. She glanced behind her and saw a bald-headed male runner who was solidly built. He reminded her of Justin, minus the hair.

She tried not to allow her imagination to run wild once again. It had already been established that her ex was nowhere to be found in Taller's Creek. Still, the mere thought of his presence had prompted her to start carrying pepper spray when running. Just as a precaution, should she ever need it.

Picking up the pace, Giselle sensed that the man on her tail had done the same. *What's his problem?* she asked herself, unnerved. Maybe that problem was her? Was his intention to attack her in broad daylight?

As panic ensued, she sucked in a deep breath and increased her speed even more as Giselle rounded a corner and trekked down the sidewalk. Glancing over her shoulder, she saw that he was still running in her direction.

And gaining ground, in spite of her best efforts to the contrary.

When it became clear to Giselle that she would not be able to outrun him and there was no one to come to her assistance, she decided to fight for her survival and freedom from victimization.

Without breaking stride, she started to reach inside the pocket of her shorts for the pepper spray—fully intending to spray it into his face liberally at the last possible moment to be most effective in catching him off guard.

But before Giselle could put her plan into action, the man had moved onto the street as though she were slowing him down, and raced past her—never even looking her way.

False alarm.

She flushed with embarrassment as Giselle caught her breath. *He wasn't out to harm me after all*, she told herself, breathing a sigh of relief while at the same time recognizing that she couldn't allow herself to be spooked by anyone who reminded her of Justin. Or was seen as threatening, unless proven otherwise.

She pushed the pepper spray deeper into her pocket and continued the run, determined to lead a normal life in Alaska, which had been given a major boost with the presence of Quincy in it. Along with his family, which gave Giselle hope that she could still have a family of her own one day.

JUSTIN TRAILED GISELLE slowly down the street in his vehicle, making sure he kept just enough of a distance to not give himself away just yet.

He had watched with interest as she'd appeared to freak out at the thought of another runner attacking her. Fortunately, the bald-headed man had passed her by harmlessly. But not before Giselle had seemed to reach into her pocket, as if prepared to pull out something in her defense. Probably pepper spray or another weapon.

She'd aborted this when the threat by the runner had proved all for naught.

I'm guessing at least part of her feared she was being stalked by me, Justin told himself, laughing at the notion. Though he had gone to extremes to keep his presence— and identity—under wraps, Justin was sure he had managed to keep Giselle uncomfortable at the mere possibility that he could have tracked her down years after she'd vanished from his life sneakily.

If that were the case, then he was happy that she continued to look over her shoulder, knowing he was never going to stop searching for her.

Now that he had found her, Giselle's fears that he would punish her for all but leaving him at the altar empty-handed were more than warranted.

The time would come soon that he would carry out his vengeance and she would sorely regret the mistake she'd made of getting on his bad side.

It tended to come at a very high price.

Justin's mind drifted to Jenna Sweeney, his former girlfriend, who'd never given him the chance to propose before bolting. When he'd caught up to her, the look in Jenna's eyes while he'd been stabbing her to death her had given him the immense satisfaction Justin had sought in that moment.

He looked forward to getting the same adrenaline rush once Giselle breathed her last breath of life.

Justin watched as his ex-fiancée turned another corner, en route to her apartment. Though tempted to follow her there and finish the job, instead he doubled down on patience and drove past the street, more than willing to wait for it to happen under his own terms.

Chapter Ten

"Ellen called in sick with a bad cold," Jill told Giselle when she walked inside Taller's Creek Books the following morning.

"Probably for the best." Giselle wrinkled her nose. "I'd hate to catch it."

"Me too." The bookstore owner sighed. "Unfortunately, with Wesley vacationing in Mexico with his girlfriend and Sadie a no-show for work, it's just us today."

Giselle was not all that surprised that the young college student had failed to come in with apparently no notification to that effect. After all, Sadie could hardly be considered dependable when she only put in a few erratic hours at the bookstore a week. As for Wesley, he and his love interest, Farrah, had been planning their trip, so his absence was expected. Ellen, who rarely missed a day, had chosen the wrong one to take off.

Giselle smiled at Jill and said lightheartedly, "We'll just have to suck it up and carry the load all by ourselves."

"You're right." Jill forced a grin and patted her hand. "Glad to know someone's capable of carrying their weight around here." She eyed Giselle enviously. "Not that there's much weight on your slender frame."

Giselle colored, taking this as a compliment. "I'm happy to be of service to you," she assured her, still mindful that Jill had given her a job when it had been most needed after arriving in Alaska under stressful circumstances. "So, what's on tap for today?"

"We need to unbox some new books that came in yesterday and shelve or table them," Jill said. "Then you can assist anyone who needs help while I do some bookkeeping."

Giselle grinned. "Sounds like a plan."

Half an hour later, Giselle was halfway through rearranging a shelf of romance novels, while thinking dreamily about Quincy and first meeting him there, when her thoughts were interrupted by a customer who needed her assistance, saying to Giselle, "Excuse me…"

The woman was in her midfifties and had light blond hair in a pompadour updo while wearing rectangle-shaped eyeglasses. Giselle couldn't help but think that she reminded her of her late mother, whose hair had been a darker shade of blond and styled differently. "How can I help you?"

Turned out that the customer needed some ideas for books to ship to her son, who had recently relocated to New Zealand for a job transfer. Giselle was more than happy to give some suggestions once she was given a bit to go on regarding the son's tastes in reading.

The woman ended up choosing half a dozen titles and couldn't wait to get the books sent off. Giselle rang them up, while envious of the obviously strong love she sensed for one's child. It was something she'd gotten from her own mother and Giselle knew she would give to her own children someday, if so blessed.

And she would equally have as much love to give to their father, if he was half the man she expected him to be. Quincy filled her head in that instant, with Justin fast becoming a distant, and largely forgettable, memory.

QUINCY AND fellow armed ABI Major Crimes Unit investigator Alan Edmonston, along with members of the Child Abuse Investigation Unit, Southcentral Area-wide Narcotics investigators and Soldotna Police Department personnel, converged on a single-story commercial building on Elder Street in Soldotna. They were backed by an AST Southcentral SWAT team equipped with Geissele Super Duty AR-15 rifles and dual-purpose K-9 troopers, excelling as both scent detection and search and rescue dogs. After a monthslong statewide investigation into human and sex trafficking that went after traffickers exploiting vulnerable Alaska Native teenagers and women—including crimes of violence and child pornography—enough hard evidence had been gathered, cooperating witnesses protected and the necessity to act now to rescue victims to move forward with the operation.

The operation went nearly without a hitch, as multiple arrests were made and victims of trafficking, some drugged or otherwise in obvious distress, were located and transported to Central Peninsula Hospital on Hospital Place for evaluation and treatment before eventually being reunited with their families. Weapons and narcotics were seized from the location, along with piles of cash and laptops. The perps would be held fully accountable for the criminality they'd engaged in.

Quincy was confident in their operation, which included arrests in other jurisdictions simultaneously with a similar degree of success across the state. These types of crimes were particularly hard to stomach and had no place in Alaska or anywhere, really. He hated the thought that his niece or nephew—or even his sister, for that matter—could be swept up in the victimization, were they in the wrong place at the wrong time. Just as excruciating would be if his own future children were exposed to such predators. Or Giselle, as another innocent person, were a trafficker able to get a jump on her. Regardless of what their own future held, though Quincy remained optimistic as to what that could be, he didn't want her to be hurt.

Alan looked at Quincy while they stood near his SUV, a satisfied look on his face. "We got them."

"Yeah." Quincy nodded. "Unfortunately there will always be others to take their places," he muttered realistically. He knew that the market for human traffickers was still ripe for perpetrators to ply their illicit trade in a vast landscape where Alaska Natives were disproportionately impacted.

"And we'll keep coming after them," Alan countered determinedly.

Kelly Reppun, the SCAN unit detective, overheard them and, while walking in their direction, asked, "What other choice is there? We're all that's standing between them and those most vulnerable to exploitation."

"You've got that right." Quincy gave her a definite nod of agreement. "We do what we need to do—for them and us." It was the only way to deal with the realities of the work they did, while knowing what was being given back to the communities they served in Alaska. "The victims will get all the support they need to work their way back from the horrors they experienced."

Kelly and Alan voiced their belief in this as well before Quincy separated from them and headed to his own SUV.

No sooner had he gotten inside when a dispatch call came in about a situation in Taller's Creek. A young woman had been found dead in the bathtub of her apartment. The circumstances were as yet undetermined.

Quincy furrowed his brow, thinking, *Never a dull moment as an ABI investigator.*

He headed out to the location and hoped afterward to drop in on Giselle at the bookstore and see if she wanted to hang out later. This was something he found himself looking more and more forward to with each passing day they got to know each other. He was sure she felt the same way, filling his heart with glee at the prospect.

MIRIAM FONTAINE WOULD HAVE just as soon started her shift any other way than discover that another young person in Taller's Creek had died before her time. Sadly, this proved all too true as the police sergeant stared at the deceased female, her ashen face matted with dark hair just above the soapy water that filled the acrylic bathtub in the apartment on Harper Lane. Pink slippers were on the porcelain tiles. A broken wineglass lay nearby on the floor, its contents of red wine spilled.

She was identified as Sadie Pisano, a twenty-one-year-old student at Kenai Peninsula College. Her head had been pulled up after being submerged in an attempt to save her life, as reported by the woman's roommate. According to Cynthia Saranillio, twenty-two and also in college, after staying overnight at her boyfriend's house, she'd returned to the apartment to find Sadie unconscious. After being unable to revive her, she'd phoned 911, frantic that her friend might be dead.

Miriam had no reason to disbelieve the roommate's story at the moment, including her insistence that Pisano would not have killed herself deliberately. To Miriam, it appeared at a glance that she might have accidentally hit her head on the tub and passed out, going under the water. Alcohol consumption might have also been a factor.

Miriam couldn't help but think about the recent local deaths of other women while wondering what were the odds against such in their small community. She requested assistance from the ABI and notified the medical examiner to get some answers.

AFTER QUINCY ARRIVED at the two-story Creeklin Apartments building and made his way to unit 117, he was greeted by Miriam Fontaine, who had a dour look on her face as they stepped inside.

"What are we looking at?" Quincy asked her knowingly while glancing about the small, neat place with contemporary furnishings and beige carpet.

"We have a college student named Sadie Pisano, dead inside her tub, while taking a bath apparently," Miriam reported levelly. "No obvious signs of foul play…"

"Okay." He followed her into the bathroom and took a look at the naked woman in the tub, who might have seemed like she was asleep were it not for her deathly coloring. Quincy took note of the broken glass of wine, which he had to consider could have been spiked with a date-rape drug or laced with fentanyl to facilitate a possible sexual assault. "Who found the body?"

"The roommate—Cynthia Saranillio—upon returning this morning, after spending the night with her boyfriend, Travis Kozuki, at his place."

"Hell of a way to discover someone you live with," Quincy muttered morosely.

"Tell me about it." Miriam jutted her chin. "She raised Sadie's head from beneath the water to try to revive her—to no avail."

Quincy didn't fault her for taking this necessary action, which could have made a difference had she gotten to the dead woman sooner. "Where's the roommate now?"

"She stepped outside."

"I'd like to talk to her," he said.

The sergeant nodded and led the way, spotting the young woman sitting on the lawn, weeping, near some cottonwood trees.

Getting her attention, Miriam said equably, "This is Trooper Lankard of the Alaska Bureau of Investigation. He needs to ask you a few more questions."

Quincy regarded the roommate, who was biracial and thinly built, with black hair with blond highlights in a collarbone-length blunt cut. Her clothes were wet from the bath water. Cynthia wiped her brown eyes and gazed up at him before he said considerately, "Ms. Saranillio, can you tell me when you last saw Sadie Pisano alive?"

"About ten last night, before I left," she answered tensely.

"And what was she doing at the time?" he wondered.

"Cramming for an exam."

It was something Quincy remembered all too well

from his own college days, which fortunately hadn't come to such a sad ending. He asked necessarily, in noting the apparent lack of forced entry, "Does anyone else have a key to your apartment?"

Cynthia blinked. "No, just me and Sadie," she contended.

"Was Ms. Pisano dating anyone?"

"No. She was single."

Quincy still couldn't rule out that there might have been someone in her life, unbeknownst to the roommate, who could have wished Sadie Pisano harm. "Did she have any enemies that you know of?"

Cynthia didn't need long to think about it. "I can't think of anyone who didn't like Sadie," she claimed.

"Was she suicidal?" he asked, thinking about Yuki Kotake's self-inflicted death.

"Definitely not!" Cynthia raised her voice. "It had to be an accident," she insisted, wiping her eyes again. "Sadie loved life, which makes it so hard to believe that this happened."

Quincy glanced at Miriam, whose expression was unreadable, and back. He knew the scene would still need to be processed by the Crime Scene Unit as part of any ABI probe of a questionable death, appearances notwithstanding.

"Did you have any inkling that Ms. Pisano might have been in trouble when you arrived at the apartment this morning?" he wondered curiously. "Had you tried to call her or anything and she wasn't picking up?"

"I did text Sadie before I left my boyfriend's place but got no response," Cynthia replied matter-of-factly. "I didn't think anything of it." She drew in a deep breath.

"But when I got here and saw her bike, I wondered why she was still home and not at work."

"Where did she work?" Quincy asked.

"Sadie worked part-time at Taller's Creek Books on Milton Lane."

Hearing that threw him for a loop, and Miriam took note of his unavoidable reaction and asked, "What is it?"

"I know someone who also works at the bookstore," he responded musingly. *Giselle must have known Sadie*, Quincy told himself uncomfortably. Just as she'd known the two other women—Neve Chenoweth and Yuki Kotake— who had died tragically and prematurely. He didn't begin to know what to make of the timing, other than purely happenstance. Sad as that was.

The state deputy medical examiner, Joslyn Bartiromo, arrived with her team to take possession of the decedent.

Doctor Bartiromo was in her midthirties and slender, with thick brunette hair in a shoulder-length cut. She was wearing nitrile exam gloves as she'd done an initial exam of Sadie Pisano's body after the tub had been drained.

"What do you think happened here?" Quincy asked her inquisitively once the corpse had been placed in a body bag and loaded onto the transport vehicle.

Joslyn smoothed an eyebrow and answered, "My initial assessment is that the decedent drowned in the bathtub, probably by accident. And possibly involved her use of alcohol." She paused, then said deliberately, "Let's see what the autopsy concludes."

With a nod, Quincy went with the likely cause of death as not involving foul play till further notice. But that wouldn't make it any easier to have to be the bearer of

bad news to Giselle. And how she might react in knowing yet another female in her orbit had died.

WHEN QUINCY WALKED into the bookstore, Giselle's heart
skipped a beat. There was no denying that he was doing
things to her that were both exhilarating and scary. She
didn't want to be hurt again. But she also didn't want to
deny herself something good—maybe very good—that
could come from being involved with the ABI trooper.

She left the stack of books on the floor to shelve and
met him halfway. "Hey there," she greeted him affably,
resisting the urge to kiss him in that setting. Maybe later.

"Hey." He looked at her ponderingly. "Do you want
to go grab a cup of coffee?"

She frowned. "I'd love to, but there's only two of us
on duty today. Our part-time help, Sadie, never came in,
so…"

"Yeah, about that—" Quincy clenched his jaw. "I'm
afraid I have some bad news to share." He paused. "Sadie
Pisano's dead."

"What?" Giselle swallowed thickly. "How?"

"She drowned in her bathtub…" He put firm hands on
Giselle's shoulders, as if she would collapse. "But before
you jump to more far off conclusions that Justin Buckner had something to do with this, the deputy medical
examiner's preliminary cause of death is that it was an
accident and that the wine Sadie Pisano was drinking
at the time was likely a factor."

Giselle got this and felt a certain sense of relief. But
that didn't prevent her from having a sense of dread. If
only because this was yet another person whom she'd

been acquainted with who'd died under mysterious—if not unlawful—circumstances, in short order.

Was this really all coincidental?

Or was there something very wrong here, in spite of the indications otherwise?

"Are you all right?" The tenderness of Quincy's words of concern did not go unnoticed by Giselle.

"I'm fine," she insisted, knowing it was incumbent upon her to show strength when faced with such terrible news. "I'll need to tell Jill Kekiwi, the bookstore owner, to let her know why Sadie was a no-show for work today," Giselle stated gloomily. "She's in her office."

"I'll go with you," Quincy insisted, "and help any way I can to answer questions she may have. Of course, I'll also assist the police, if necessary, in notifying Ms. Pisano's family about her passing."

"All right. Let's go talk to Jill."

Giselle liked that he was there for her during challenging times. This surely qualified as such. Even if Sadie's death had nothing to do with Justin and his sick obsession with her, which Giselle had to believe was now a thing of the past.

JUSTIN STRAINED HIMSELF while going for one hundred–plus push-ups at his rented farmhouse. It was just one of the ways he kept himself going while hiding in plain view in Alaska. Other ways included getting high.

Then there was cold-blooded murder.

He imagined by now that the body of his latest victim had been discovered. It wasn't especially difficult to charm his way into her life in secret, lulling her into a false sense of security before snuffing out her existence and making it seem like an accident of her own making.

Or anything that didn't point back at him.

Just like the other two women who'd happened to know Giselle. And paid for it.

Giselle herself would be punished soon enough for thinking that escape was ever in the cards for her. Not in this lifetime. It had always been only a matter of time before he'd found out where she'd been hiding. And dispensed the type of retaliation that she wouldn't soon forget.

He laughed at the wicked thought before focusing on his workout and building up the muscles on his body that would serve him well at the end of the day in staying one step ahead of the authorities.

And two steps or more behind Giselle. Till they had one final face-to-face encounter.

Chapter Eleven

On Wednesday afternoon, Giselle got together with her friend, Jacinta Cruz, for a drink at the Owl's Den bar on Ninth Street in Taller's Creek. She had met the Latina award-winning producer of documentaries on Alaska culture and history through Neve. Jacinta was tall, thin and attractive, with bold blue eyes and long blond hair in face-framing flippy layers that reminded Giselle of a style hers used to be.

They sat on wooden stools at the bar, sipping margaritas while commiserating over the unexpected deaths of their friends, Neve and Yuki.

Jacinta furrowed her brow. "I still can't believe they're gone."

"I know, right?" Giselle frowned thoughtfully. "It seems unreal."

"Doesn't it always?" Jacinta agreed, tasting her drink. "They will always be a part of our lives in spirit."

Giselle believed this too, but it was hardly the same as being there in the flesh. As if this wasn't enough to stomach, she had to add to the tragedies by relaying the untimely passing of her coworker at the bookstore, Sadie Pisano.

"Sadie died while taking a bath," she said. "Apparently hit her head, went under and never came up."

"I'm so sorry," Jacinta expressed. She put her hand on Giselle's. "They say that bad things come in threes. If true, then maybe the bad karma you've had to endure has run its course."

"I sure hope so." Giselle gave a little smile and sipped on the margarita. As it was, three people dying in the prime of their lives were three too many. Or would there be more deaths to come of people she knew? She hated to even think about the notion, wanting only to get past this dark period and move on with her life.

"Okay, enough with the negativity," Jacinta said, taking a sip of her drink. "Let's move on to more positive things…such as your love life. Any news you care to share on that front? I know you haven't really been in the market for anything too serious since you arrived in Alaska…"

"Actually, I'm seeing a state trooper right now," Giselle was happy to announce, seeing no reason to keep this a secret among friends who asked.

"Seriously?" Jacinta's eyes popped wide. "Since when?"

"Since he showed up at the bookstore recently and we struck up a conversation. It went from there." Giselle spared her the details of Quincy's investigation into Neve's death that had led him to Taller's Creek Books that day.

"I'm so happy for you." Jacinta flashed her teeth. "Hope your trooper turns out to be everything you'd like him to be."

"So do I," Giselle told her and added spiritedly, "So far, so good." She knew that was an understatement.

Quincy had almost proven to be too good to be true, but she saw nothing that would dampen that view of him. And only wanted to be just as desirable as a romantic partner, and more, to him. "What about you? Any prospects on the dating scene?" she asked Jacinta, who had been married once briefly at a young age but was currently single.

"I wish." Jacinta rolled her eyes. "The good ones are hard to come by these days. But hey, if your trooper knows any single and good-looking troopers on the market, send them my way."

Giselle laughed. "Will do." From what she'd gathered from Quincy, most of his coworkers with the ABI were spoken for in one way or another. But it couldn't hurt to ask. So long as she kept him for herself—which, thankfully, he seemed more than amenable to.

After finishing her cocktail, Giselle left Jacinta at the bar and headed home to feed Muffin and do some chores. Quincy was planning to drop by for dinner and whatever else they decided to do with their time together.

JUSTIN WAITED, staying out of Giselle's line of vision— not wanting to chance her recognizing him, even with a new look, in an open setting—for her to leave the Owl's Den bar. Admittedly, a part of him had wanted to spring on her like a thief in the night, undoubtedly shaking his onetime fiancée to the core. But that would take away the element of surprise, while exposing his secret presence in Alaska prematurely.

That might not go well in the long run, as he dodged the authorities who were investigating him back in Chesapeake. He had no desire to tip them off as to his whereabouts that Justin was sure would capture their interests sooner than later.

So, instead, he remained in the shadows at a back table, sipping on a gin and tonic, gazing at Giselle as she walked out the door. *See you soon, my love—take that to the bank*, he thought sarcastically as he finished off the drink and got to his feet.

Justin coolly approached the woman Giselle had been chatting with at the bar. She was talking on her cell phone. He recognized her from the candlelight vigil he had attended to honor Neve Chenoweth, the first local and acquaintance of Giselle's that Justin had taken out and gotten away with.

Sitting on the stool beside Jacinta Cruz, he waited till the nice-looking woman had gotten off the phone before Justin put on his deceptive charm and best smile. After which he said smoothly, "Can I buy the beautiful lady another drink?" Not waiting for her to respond, he added, "I just hate drinking all by myself—"

"So do I," she told him, blushing all the while. "You're welcome to buy me a drink, if you insist."

"I do." He ordered two margaritas and hit her with a totally captivated look, then said dishonestly, "By the way, my name's Jesse Teague."

"Jacinta Cruz."

No kidding, Justin mused sardonically, as he was already on top of this, but offered sweetly, "Very nice to make your acquaintance."

QUINCY WAS AT his desk when he got the request for a video chat from Daniel Malaterre, his friend with the FBI. He accepted and said, "Hey, Daniel."

"Quincy." Daniel was all business in his expression. "Have some news on Justin Buckner I thought might be of interest to you…and your friend—"

"Okay…" Quincy tuned in for what he had to say.

"Wanted to let you know that Buckner's office and home were raided early this morning and troves of evidence confiscated as part of the investigation into him."

"That's good," Quincy couldn't help but say, knowing that putting the man out of commission would certainly be comforting to Giselle. "What about Buckner himself? Has he been arrested yet?"

Creases appeared on Daniel's forehead as he said, "Afraid not. Based on what they found—or didn't—it appears as though he may have skipped town, perhaps had an inkling that things were about to turn south for him and left in a hurry."

Quincy muttered an expletive, frowning. "Not what I wanted to hear."

"Figured as much." Daniel jutted his chin. "A warrant has been issued for Buckner's arrest and a BOLO alert has been put out for his blue BMW 430i coupe." He drew a breath. "My guess is he could be anywhere, but he won't get very far." He spoke confidently.

"What about Alaska?" Quincy asked point-blank. He thought about Giselle and the extraordinary means she'd gone through to get away from that creep. Could he have actually discovered her whereabouts? And come after her, his legal issues notwithstanding?

"Highly unlikely," Daniel stressed. "That's a long way from Virginia, and as yet, there's no reason to believe he's gone to Alaska to escape his troubles. Or expose himself by stalking an ex-fiancée."

"I'm sure you're right." Quincy was inclined to agree, all things considered. "Keep me posted."

"Sure thing."

He signed off, and Quincy mused about Buckner, wondering where he was holed up and just how long it would take for the feds to dig him out.

LATER, WHILE IN BED and after he'd pleasured Giselle and been satisfied by her in kind during their lovemaking, Quincy cuddled her to his body and said evenly, "So, I thought you'd like to know that Buckner's house and office were raided this morning—making good on the feds' plans to go after him…"

Giselle raised her eyes at Quincy expectantly. "Justin's in custody?"

"Not yet, unfortunately," he hated to admit. "But a warrant has been issued for his arrest, and with any luck, Buckner will be behind bars before you know it." Quincy hoped that would be enough reassurance that she had nothing to be worried about.

"Okay." Giselle sighed. "The sooner, the better."

"I agree," he told her. "And I can promise you the feds feel exactly the same way. They take the types of white-collar crimes Buckner's being charged with seriously."

"Good."

Just as Quincy had taken the moment of pacification as an excuse to kiss Giselle, Muffin suddenly jumped up onto the bed, seemingly determined to command their attention.

With a chuckle, Quincy lifted up the playful kitten and said, "Looks like someone feels threatened that I'm muscling in on her territory."

"Probably." Giselle laughed. "I think there's enough of me to go around for the two of you."

Quincy grinned and said, "Try convincing her of that."

"She'll just have to learn over time," Giselle insisted, taking the kitten out of his hands. She kissed the top of Muffin's head and said, "Now, be a good little kitten and give us some space." She released her, and Muffin seemed to take the hint, hopping off the bed and racing out of the room.

"Now, where were we...?" Giselle asked Quincy in a sexual tone of voice, nibbling on his lips with hers.

"You tell me. Or, better yet, show me," he replied teasingly into her mouth, and Quincy felt his libido uptick once again, in what he felt had to be the first stages of true love. If they weren't already well beyond that point.

THE FOLLOWING MORNING at work, Quincy got the autopsy report on Sadie Pisano's death. Reading with interest, he expected it to more or less confirm the preliminary assessment of the deputy medical examiner that the death had likely been accidental drowning.

Instead, as he sat at his desk, Quincy found the official conclusion to the contrary. According to Dr. Rhonda Ullerup, the chief medical examiner, the college student had died from drowning, but she'd determined the manner of death to be a homicide. She described bruising on the decedent's arms and shoulders, consistent with being held down in the bathtub water against the victim's will.

Equally disturbing to Quincy in the report was reading that Sadie Pisano had ingested the drug GHB, which had likely made her dizzy or unconscious and contributed to her death, in spite of a lack of evidence of a sexual assault. He strongly suspected that the substance had been put in the wine she'd drunk that night, which would undoubtedly be detected by the crime lab's Blood and Beverage Alcohol Section once the Crime Scene Unit's investigation of what had actually turned out to be a crime scene had been completed.

So, Sadie Pisano was killed by someone, Quincy thought, sitting back, unnerved at the sudden turn in the dynamics. Who was the unsub? Had Sadie known her killer? Was anyone else in danger?

Since Giselle was an employee of the same bookstore Sadie had worked at, he could only wonder if there could be any logical connection that could put her at risk.

While pondering this unsettling thought, Quincy took out his cell phone and updated Taller's Creek PD Sergeant Miriam Fontaine with the news.

To SAY IT WAS business as usual at Taller's Creek Books would be a real stretch. Certainly, this was the way Giselle saw it, as they were still reeling over the death of one of their own. No one really wanted to talk about Sadie's passing, but it was surely on everyone's mind. That included Wesley, who had offered to cut short his vacation to return to work, knowing they were grieving and shorthanded—but Jill had insisted it wasn't necessary. Ellen, who had overcome her cold and was back, agreed.

As did Giselle, who only wanted to keep busy and try to keep things as normal as possible but was finding that difficult, to say the least. Though she hadn't known Sadie that well, losing her, even in an accident, hurt. Especially after two other females in Giselle's circle had died prematurely.

I can't control what I can't control, she told herself while arranging books on a table.

A few minutes later, Giselle could tell when Quincy came into the bookstore that something weighed heavily on his mind. Had she become that intuitive about the man she was romantically involved with? Maybe so, which she considered to be a good thing for where this seemed to be headed. She wondered if he too felt he could read her like a book.

"There's been a development..." He spoke in a somber tone, clearly there in an official capacity.

"What is it?" Giselle met his eyes tensely.

"Maybe it's best that I speak to all the employees here at once."

Now you're scaring me, she mused, ill at ease, but said, "All right."

After stepping with him into the back room, where Jill and Ellen were talking shop while surrounded by stacks of books and boxes, Giselle got their attention and said to Ellen, "This is Quincy Lankard, with the Alaska Bureau of Investigation. He has something to say to us."

"Must be serious," Jill remarked, touching her glasses.

Quincy stood in the middle of the three of them and said straightforwardly, "Sadie Pisano's death has been ruled a homicide..."

"What?" Ellen's mouth hung open.

"It wasn't an accidental drowning?" Giselle followed in disbelief.

"Not according to the chief medical examiner," Quincy said flatly.

Jill peered at him. "Do you have any suspects?"

He eyed Giselle, and she sensed that he was reading

her thoughts—or more specifically, fears resurfacing about Justin and his threats—before Quincy answered succinctly, "None as yet. But the current working theory is that Ms. Pisano may have had a stalker, either from her college environment or while working here at the bookstore. Perhaps the orange roses delivered here were meant for her. We're pursuing all angles at the moment."

Someone might have been stalking Sadie? Giselle thought. Ending with her murder? This was certainly not implausible, she believed, having assumed the roses were for herself. She should have considered that any of the bookstore employees could have been targeted and not just her.

Giselle looked at Quincy and asked curiously, "What other angles are you pursuing...?"

He pinched his nose while pondering the question. "We're looking into the possibility that it could have been a random attack. Or a crime of passion or opportunity. Even a case of mistaken identity." Quincy paused. "Though there's probably nothing to worry about, the association with Ms. Pisano through the bookstore can't be dismissed altogether, per se. As such, I would suggest that you watch your backs to be on the safe side. Till the case is solved."

Giselle stiffened at the thought, knowing that for better or worse, Quincy was giving them a clear warning that perhaps a deranged book lover was behind Sadie's death.

Or could there be more cause for concern that whoever had killed her had other ulterior motives?

Chapter Twelve

In Nobber's Hill, Virginia, forty miles outside of Chesapeake, Chad and Suzanna Zimmerman were walking their black Cane Corso named Klay through a wooded area near South Blebard Highway. A month removed from celebrating their fiftieth wedding anniversary, they looked forward to being joined by their children and grandchildren for a big celebration to mark the occasion.

For her part, Suzanna relished the thought of being with Chad way back when they'd been attending the University of Virginia in Charlottesville as college freshmen—and had become practically inseparable ever since. Now in their seventies, she wondered just how long they could keep it going before one or the other ran out of steam.

She decided it did no good to dwell on the negative. Especially when there was still so much to look forward to.

That included the companionship of their dog, who seemed to adore them every bit as much as they did him.

Suzanna was holding the leash, giving Chad a break, when Klay suddenly tried to break away, causing her to nearly lose her grip. He obviously was attracted to something. Perhaps an object that captured his fancy, as was often the case during their walks.

"You see something, Klay?" she asked curiously.

Chad noticed too and asked, "What is it, boy?" He took control of the leash and allowed the dog to get to where it wanted to go.

Suzanna, with her arthritic knees, struggled to keep up with them. But when she did get to the spot where Klay was digging his paws into the dirt, she froze as she saw something no one should ever have to see.

What was clearly the skeletal remains of a human being was being unearthed before Suzanna's horrified eyes.

QUINCY HAD REALLY hated to lay that bit of bad news on Giselle and her coworkers an hour ago. But there'd been no easy way to say that Sadie Pisano had been a victim of foul play. And that the killer was still at large.

He wanted to dismiss the notion that the victimization was related to Taller's Creek Books. Much less, Giselle in particular. But Quincy was concerned about the orange roses delivered to the bookstore by an anonymous so-called book lover. Was this a forerunner to Sadie's murder? Or entirely unrelated?

That's what I need to find out, Quincy told himself as he pulled up to Ruby's Flowers and Gifts on Lavender Way.

Stepping inside the florist shop, he approached a sixtysomething female employee with short crimson hair as she was arranging a bouquet of red ranunculus and sunflowers.

She looked up at him with a smile and asked, "Can I help you with something?"

"I hope so." Quincy identified himself as an ABI investigator. "I need some information on the person who bought a dozen orange roses recently and had them delivered to Taller's Creek Books…"

"I remember that," she said matter-of-factly. "We don't get as many customers wanting to send orange roses, as opposed to red, pink or even purple. I recall that the gentleman was pretty specific in what he wanted sent to the bookstore."

"Do you remember if he used a credit card to pay for the roses?"

"He paid in cash," she said flatly.

Quincy frowned. "What can you tell me about the man?"

"Not much, I'm afraid. He was white, tall and…oh yes, I believe he was wearing a cap."

"About how old was he?" Quincy asked.

"Thirties, I'd guess but can't really say for sure. I've never been very good at guessing ages." She eyed him curiously. "What's he done?"

"Perhaps nothing," Quincy admitted. *Or maybe committed murder*, he mused. "Just routine stuff as part of an ongoing criminal investigation."

"I see. Sorry I couldn't be more help."

Me too, Quincy thought but told her, "Have a nice day."

Back in his vehicle, he pondered which angles to pursue next in tracking down who might have killed the college student. And whether or not there was more to the story than met the eye.

GISELLE SAT IN the café, nibbling on a honey-almond granola bar while sipping coffee. She was still reeling over the news that Sadie had been murdered—perhaps by someone who'd been stalking her.

Would Quincy get to the bottom of it?

Or would the killer remain on the loose, while possibly targeting others?

The thought was chilling to Giselle, but she took solace in knowing that the ABI was handling the investigation and that Quincy seemed intent on solving the crime. As well as allaying her own fears that Justin was somehow in the mix, even if he seemed to have his hands full at the moment while trying to evade the law.

Stop it, Giselle admonished herself as she took another bite of the granola bar. She lifted her cell phone from the table and saw that Jacinta had sent her a text.

Hey, met a new guy named Jesse. Cool to hang out with. Wish me luck!

Giselle grinned. She was happy for her friend and did hope that things worked out with this guy. Just as she wanted her own relationship with Quincy to blossom. Definitely seemed like they were headed in the right direction.

But then, she once believed that was the case with Justin. And look where that had gotten her.

In fact, it had gotten her to Alaska. And eventually into Quincy's bed. With him also being in her bed. It had to mean something special. Right?

Giselle sipped more coffee thoughtfully before heading back to the bookstore.

JUSTIN STOOD ABOVE the king-size bed, staring at the woman he'd just had sex with. Jacinta was naked and asleep as she lay on the crumpled sheet, having exhausted herself just as he had.

Though he'd enjoyed being with her somewhat—and other women too in recent years for consensual sex—it was only because he was fantasizing about Giselle while going through the motions and physical release. But that could only last so long. There was no substitute for the real thing.

Or, in this case, the woman who was still in his dreams. Even if Giselle had abandoned him. He hadn't abandoned her. Not really. She would be his again. At least in theory.

In reality, Giselle's utter betrayal would come at a price she could never walk away from. He wouldn't let her. How could he and live with himself?

Any more than when Jenna had betrayed him and forced a reaction from him that she'd lived to regret. Or *died* was more like it.

Justin peered at his latest bedmate. He knew this would be short-lived before it ran its course. Then he would do what needed to be done.

He felt added pressure in knowing that the feds were on his trail, having raided his office and home and put out a warrant for his arrest. By the time they figured out his whereabouts, he would be long gone, safely to someplace out of the country.

But until such time, there was Giselle to deal with. And that he would.

You'll get what's coming to you, Justin told himself single-mindedly of his ex-fiancée.

He watched as Jacinta stirred a bit before curling into a fetal position and snoring lightly. Leaving the room,

Justin lit up a joint and weighed his next move in what had become a deadly game of cat and pretty mouse, where there could only be one winner at the end of the day.

ON SATURDAY, Quincy was at his desk when Daniel Malaterre phoned for a video chat, which he quickly accepted.

"Hey," Quincy said.

"Got some unsettling news for you," Daniel uttered equably, frowning. "First, we located Justin's Buckner's BMW in a long-term parking garage near Norfolk International Airport, suggesting that he's fled the state of Virginia."

"That's too bad," Quincy muttered, even if he'd already believed this to be a distinct possibility. It still riled him, though, knowing that the longer Buckner remained at large, the greater the threat to Giselle's peace of mind.

"Gets worse, I'm afraid." Daniel's brows lowered and he sighed. "Two days ago, human remains were discovered partially buried in the woods in Nobber's Hill, Virginia, about forty miles from Chesapeake. Dental records and the clothing worn were used to identify the badly decomposed adult female as Jenna Sweeney, the twenty-six-year-old waitress who vanished four years ago without a trace. Till now." He jutted his chin. "An autopsy on the skeletal remains indicated she was stabbed to death by someone…"

Before he could complete his news, Quincy's heart skipped a beat while blurting out instinctively, "Justin Buckner—"

Daniel's countenance was expressionless as he replied calmly, "A latent print found on the eyeglasses of the victim was submitted to the Bureau's Integrated Automated Fingerprint Identification System. There was a hit. The fingerprint matched Buckner's as an arrestee in the database. It was enough for the Chesapeake Police Department to issue a new warrant for his arrest for murder. There's now a nationwide manhunt underway to bring him in."

"Do you have any clue as to where Buckner might be hiding?" Quincy asked anxiously.

"Not really. We've had reports that he might have been spotted in Delaware, Massachusetts, Michigan, New York, Nebraska—even as far away as California and Nevada," Daniel said. "He may have managed to get out of the country, given that he was able to drain his bank accounts before taking off. We're checking the airlines, trains and other means Buckner could be using to stay on the run."

Quincy drew a sharp breath. "I'd hate to think that Buckner could have somehow made his way to Alaska," he expressed fearfully, musing about Giselle.

"I doubt that—but we'll catch him." Daniel leaned forward. "You worried about your friend?"

"Actually, she's more than a friend," Quincy admitted and thought, *We've gotten way past the friendship level*. He wouldn't have had it any other way. "We've been seeing each other."

"I see." Daniel smiled. "That's cool." He got serious again. "Buckner will be in police custody in no time flat," he insisted. "In the meantime, just keep an eye on your girlfriend."

"Will do," Quincy assured him before disconnecting. He sat back and considered that there was no reason at this time to hyperventilate over Buckner coming after someone he presumably hasn't seen in years to settle old scores. Especially when he had new concerns that should occupy all his attention.

Still, Quincy didn't relish the thought of having to tell Giselle that her ex was now wanted for the murder of Jenna Sweeney, in addition to his other alleged crimes. Fortunately, Giselle had been able to escape Buckner's homicidal tendencies.

To Quincy, this proved in and of itself that meeting her had been meant to be. He would be damned if he allowed anyone from her past—especially Justin Buckner—to ruin what Quincy believed he and Giselle could have to work with in the future.

GISELLE SAT ON the bench with Quincy in Soldotna Creek Park on States Avenue. The stunning 13.6-acre park was not far from his house and offered a breathtaking view of the Kenai River. As she gazed at it, Giselle thought maudlinly about the annual Kenai River Festival, a three-day summertime music event, which she'd attended last year with friends, including Neve and Yuki—enjoying live music, a beer and wine garden, delectable food and crafts, and more. She couldn't believe that they were no longer around to enjoy what life had to offer on the Kenai Peninsula and beyond.

When Quincy broke the silence and suggested they take a walk along the riverfront boardwalk, Giselle agreed, holding hands as they did so.

After a moment or two, he said tentatively, "So, I was speaking to my friend with the FBI, and he passed along some info regarding your ex-fiancé."

"Has Justin been arrested?" she asked, the thought of him being in handcuffs and no longer able to bilk clients or pose a threat to her exhilarating.

"No—not yet, I'm afraid." Quincy paused and tightened the grip of his fingers around her hand. "But there's even more reason now why that's imperative…"

"What are you talking about?" Giselle demanded, sensing he was stalling whatever was on his mind but it had to be serious.

"Human remains belonging to a female were discovered a couple of days ago in a wooded area of Nobber's Hill, Virginia," Quincy told her. "The victim was identified as Jenna Sweeney, the waitress I told you about who disappeared four years ago. She'd been stabbed to death." He took a ragged breath. "A fingerprint found on the eyeglasses the victim was wearing when buried in a shallow grave belongs to Justin Buckner—"

Giselle swallowed unevenly in meeting Quincy's eyes. "Are you saying that Justin killed her…?"

"The police and FBI believe this to be the case," he answered straightforwardly. "Another warrant has been issued for Buckner's arrest—for murder!"

Her heart skipped a beat as a number of thoughts rolled through Giselle's mind. How could she have fallen for someone capable of murder? What signs had she missed, beyond the obvious, that could have warned her not to get involved with him?

But most importantly in the present sense, she wondered if Justin had stopped at the killing of Jenna Sweeney. Or had he targeted others as well?

Such as Sadie, Giselle thought with dread. "What if Justin is here in Alaska after all?" she posed to Quincy while thinking about the sightings she imagined of her ex in Taller's Creek. "And made good on his threats to me—by murdering Sadie…?"

"I thought of that," Quincy told her candidly. "More than once. But it's still a big leap from Buckner allegedly killing someone years ago to showing up in Alaska out of the blue to kill your friend as a way to get back at you. Not sure Buckner is capable or cold-blooded enough to pull it off—all while dodging the authorities on other fronts."

"I hope you're right." Giselle calmed down. The last thing she wanted was to believe that Justin had become a serial killer as part of his vendetta against her, whom he was saving for last. Not that she would ever underestimate his ability to be cruel and callous to anyone who got on his bad side to one degree or another.

Especially her.

If you even think about ever leaving me, Giselle, just know that you'll pay for it in ways you can't even imagine. I'll go after everyone you care about…or cares about you, even a little…one by one. Saving you for last.

Giselle forced herself to erase the frightening words from her head. She was sure that Justin would be taken into custody at any time now to be held accountable for his growing list of crimes.

"You okay?" Quincy asked, breaking through her reverie.

"Yeah." She flashed a tiny smile.

He smiled back, looking relieved. "Good."

Just then, Giselle's cell phone buzzed. She removed it from the back pocket of her jeans. There was a text message from Seth Lombrozo, the architect whom she'd met through Yuki and Neve.

After reading it, Giselle regarded Quincy ill at ease and said with a catch to her voice, "A friend of mine, Jacinta Cruz, has gone missing—"

Chapter Thirteen

Hey, met a new guy named Jesse. Cool to hang out with. Wish me luck!

Quincy read the text again that Jacinta Cruz had sent Giselle two days earlier. *So, who the hell is this Jesse?* he wondered. And was this new guy she'd met the reason that Jacinta had been missing for a day, at least—after failing to show up at a production meeting? Without calling anyone she knew with an explanation?

Does this have anything to do with the murder of Sadie Pisano? Quincy asked himself as he peered at Giselle. She was understandably fearful for her friend's safety. And since the disappearance was apparently uncharacteristic for the documentary-film producer, Giselle had every reason to be concerned. With each passing hour that Jacinta Cruz failed to demonstrate that she was alive and well, it was becoming more likely she was either being held against her will or was the victim of foul play.

But rather than dwell on the obvious, which Quincy was certain that Giselle had pondered without his help, he said to her after they had gotten into his SUV, "Do you know anything else about Jesse?"

"Only what Jacinta said in the text," she responded and took a deep breath. "Do you think he abducted her...?"

"Possibly." He started the Ford Police Interceptor. "It's also possible that, for whatever reason, Jacinta lost track of time after telling you that she enjoyed hanging out with the man."

"I hope it's as simple as that," Giselle muttered nervously. "It's just so weird—and so unlike her—that Jacinta would leave everyone hanging as to what she's up to. Especially after what happened to Neve and Yuki—"

I'm sensing that too, Quincy told himself instinctively but said calmly, "Let's not go jumping to any conclusions just yet."

"I'm trying not to, but it isn't easy to look at the glass half full, especially when Jacinta's other friends are also worried about her," Giselle argued, wringing her hands from the passenger seat.

"When did you last actually talk to her?" he wondered.

"On Wednesday afternoon... We met for a drink at the Owl's Den bar on Ninth Street in Taller's Creek."

Quincy glanced at her. "Did anyone hit on her while you were there?"

Giselle thought about it and replied, "Not when I was with her." She paused. "But I left the bar while she was still there, talking to someone from work on her cell phone."

"So, it's possible that Jacinta could have met someone—this Jesse—there and one thing led to another... Including her disappearance."

"Yeah, I suppose." Giselle looked at him. "Maybe we should ask someone at the place, as it's not too far from here."

Quincy nodded. "I was just about to suggest the same thing." As the Taller's Creek PD had yet to officially request the assistance of the ABI in this situation, he saw no reason why she couldn't accompany him there. Especially if it led to finding her friend, safe and sound. He made a right turn at the light and headed toward the Owl's Den bar.

"THAT'S THE BARTENDER who served us," Giselle pointed out when they stepped inside the bar that was mostly empty.

"Let's see what he has to say," Quincy voiced.

They approached the fiftysomething burly man with a receding, slicked-back gray hairline ending in a short ponytail. He was stacking bottles of beer behind the bar.

"Hi," the bartender said coolly when he looked their way.

After Quincy introduced himself as working for the ABI and flashed his identification, Giselle asked, "Remember me?"

"Sure." The bartender nodded. "You and the other pretty lady came in earlier this week for drinks."

"Right—Wednesday afternoon." Giselle offered him a soft smile. "After I left, do you happen to remember if my friend—her name is Jacinta—met with anyone else...?"

"Yeah," he answered firmly, without needing to give it some thought. "A dude who had been sitting at a table by himself came over and sat next to her. They struck up a conversation and may have left together—I'm not sure."

Giselle sighed and said sharply, "My friend is missing."

The bartender cocked a thick brow. "Really?"

"Yes, and we just need to find her," she stressed.

Quincy asked him evenly, "Can you describe the man?"

The bartender pondered this and replied, "He was white, bald, maybe in his thirties and looked to be in pretty good shape."

The person described didn't ring a bell to Giselle. Not that she would expect it to, if this was the same new guy that Jacinta had texted her about. "Did you happen to catch his name?" she asked.

The bartender shook his head. "Sorry."

"How about Jesse?" Quincy prodded.

"You know, come to think of it, that might have been the name he gave her," the bartender suggested after a moment or two.

"Do you have surveillance video I can take a look at for that day?" Quincy asked.

The bartender responded sourly, "We only keep it for twenty-four hours—meaning we no longer have video from Wednesday. Sorry."

Quincy bit back disappointment and muttered, "It was worth a try."

After they left the bar, Giselle told him, "That has to be the man Jacinta is with. Or at least was with…"

"I agree," Quincy said. "The only question is is she with him voluntarily or against her will?"

Or has he killed her? Giselle had to consider with dread while wondering as well if Jacinta's mysterious disappearance could have anything to do with Sadie's death.

TWO HOURS LATER, Giselle had joined some of Jacinta's other friends on the Pippen Trail, after the documentary maker had reportedly been spotted there in the past twenty-four hours in the company of a bald-headed man.

Hey, met a new guy named Jesse. Cool to hang out with. Wish me luck!

Jacinta's text flashed in Giselle's mind as she contemplated whether the man had actually meant her harm and been deceptive in his ability to charm her friend into trusting him. Giselle couldn't help but think about once being in the same boat with Justin. At least she had survived to correct her huge error in judgment.

Could Jacinta say the same? Or had her fate already been sealed?

"This feels like déjà vu," Seth Lombrozo moaned as they searched for their missing friend through the boreal forest.

"That's what I'm afraid of," Giselle admitted. She looked sadly at Seth, who was a hulking man with a full head of dark hair and a Garibaldi beard. She thought about poor Neve and how it all had ended when her body had been discovered on the trail. Would Jacinta be next?

"Let's not jump to any premature conclusions," warned Kimberly Herrington, an up-and-coming local artist, who was petite and had red hair in a butterfly cut. "Just because Jacinta was hanging out on the trail doesn't mean she didn't go elsewhere, with or without someone accompanying her."

"Kimberly's right," Ethan Gladstone, a tall caterer with a blond fade mohawk, said. "We're all just freaking out over the worst-case scenario. She may be injured out here and unable to communicate but otherwise still very much alive."

"We have to believe that's the case," said kennel owner Pablo Wersching, who was long limbed with long brown hair parted in the middle. "Or maybe Jacinta is safe and sound, can explain where she's been and will have a good laugh at all the fuss about her."

Giselle smiled at the thought. "That would definitely be the best outcome for everyone."

"You can say that again," Kimberly uttered.

Giselle wanted desperately to believe that to be true. But she couldn't shake the notion that Jacinta was in danger—or worse—with this Jesse likely the root cause. Still, she remained hopeful as they continued to move through the rugged trail and said to the group, "Let's just see what the search and rescue operation under-way discovers—or not...assuming we come up empty-handed—"

At this point, Giselle felt that was the best they could hope for, while knowing that Quincy had been officially brought on by the Taller's Creek Police Department to lend his expertise in trying to locate Jacinta, dead or alive.

"THEY DON'T pay us enough for this," complained Gabe McAuliffe, the AST search and rescue coordinator at the command center in the quest to locate Jacinta Cruz. It included search teams on the ground, by air and an Alaska State Troopers K-9 unit.

"The pay is less important than the end result," Quincy countered. "Finding missing persons alive is in-valuable by its very nature." Even if it didn't always work out that way, he firmly believed that doing their jobs to achieve the best possible results was payment enough.

Miriam Fontaine concurred. "Until there's clear evidence of foul play here, we have to assume that Ms. Cruz is not dead but maybe just injured or lost and waiting to be found. To that end we issued a BOLO for the missing woman's orange Toyota 4Runner, which may have gone off-road."

Gabe said equably, "As always, we'll keep at it till we have some answers—one way or another."

Quincy hoped that should this turn out to be a disastrous outcome, Giselle would be able to get past it. He knew that she had joined some of Jacinta's friends as volunteer searchers, desperately wanting to find her safe and sound. Under other circumstances, he would have been right beside Giselle, holding her hand in a show of support. But he was needed elsewhere and was sure she understood.

Miriam received information over the radio, drawing Quincy's and Gabe's attention as she uttered, "They've found something…"

Gabe got the word from dispatch at the same time, in which they were told that an injured brown bear had been found just off the Pippen Trail—but no sign of Jacinta. "Keep searching," he ordered keenly.

Quincy found this news to be both a relief and disappointment and said, "She's out there somewhere. We'll find her…"

Miriam twisted her lips. "Well, we better make it sooner than later," she warned. "With dangerous wildlife like brown bears to contend with in the woods, along with human predators, if she's still alive, we have to get to her."

Gabe jutted his chin. "Maybe the volunteer searcher who helped lead us to Neve Chenoweth can work his magic again—if he's among the searchers—in tracking down Jacinta Cruz."

"So, who's this miracle worker?" Quincy asked him curiously.

"Just a guy who said he had a nose for this sort of thing and was able to point us in the right direction in finding Ms. Chenoweth," Gabe said. "Never caught his name."

Quincy was thoughtful as he asked, "What did he look like?"

Gabe contemplated this for a moment. "White, thirty-something, tall and fit, with short blond hair and blue eyes," he said as someone who was adept in attention to detail in his profession.

Taking mental notes, Quincy asked, "Did you ever see him after that?"

Gabe nodded. "As a matter of fact, I did. Saw him in town." He paused. "But he had changed his look."

"How so?" Miriam asked before Quincy could.

"He had shaved his head bald and allowed some hair to grow on his face." Gabe scratched his chin. "To tell you the truth, I almost didn't recognize him, were it not for the cold blue eyes that gave the man away."

Warning bells rang in Quincy's head like an alarm. Had the man in question led searchers to a body he'd known in advance had been on the trail, as if he had left Neve there to die?

Quincy considered that the bald-headed version of

the volunteer searcher matched the man named Jesse who'd been hitting on Jacinta at the bar. Were they one and the same?

Equally disturbing was the thought that he could also have been the same man who'd had orange roses delivered to the bookstore. Which had happened to be where Sadie Pisano had worked part-time, before someone had murdered her.

Is there some symmetry here? Quincy asked himself, ill at ease. Were they looking at a killer—maybe a serial killer—in their midst? Masquerading as one of the good guys?

If so, Quincy feared that this didn't bode well for Jacinta's survival, wherever she was.

Chapter Fourteen

By Sunday afternoon, the official search for Jacinta Cruz on the Pippen Trail had been pared down after an alleged second sighting of the documentary-film producer in another location at a later point in the time line. Though still considered missing under suspicious circumstances, there was a lack of hard evidence to clearly indicate she was in harm's way.

Quincy believed otherwise, especially with the likelihood that the last person Jacinta had been seen with, a man named Jesse, was apparently the one who'd found Neve Chenoweth. And might have sent flowers to Taller's Creek Books, where Sadie Pisano, the murdered college student, had worked—with her killer still on the loose. Where did this leave Jacinta?

We need to find this Jesse—and interrogate him, Quincy thought while standing in his great room staring out the window. And find Jacinta, hopefully still alive, if she was being held by him against her will. He knew that Giselle was at work, if only to take her mind off her latest friend's disappearance—till news came of her whereabouts. Unfortunately, at this point, with each passing hour that they failed to locate Jacinta Cruz,

Quincy recognized the greater the chance that she was no longer alive to reunite with those in her professional and personal circles.

When his cell phone buzzed, he lifted it from his pants pocket and saw that it was a call from his mother. That usually meant both parents were calling to check on him, as they were prone to do whenever they hadn't heard from him in a while. Unless one or the other had a problem to share that his sister was not privy to or kept to herself. He suspected that it was more likely that they wanted to see how things were progressing between him and Giselle. She'd left a most favorable impression on them, and he suspected that, in their minds, the next logical step was for him to marry her and give them more grandchildren to teach about the Eyak culture and more.

While he hadn't thought quite that far ahead, Quincy had thought far enough to know that he really had fallen for Giselle and wanted things to work between them in every way possible. But he needed to know she felt entirely the same way before he took things too far to the next level.

Answering the call, Quincy said sweetly, "Hey."

He had only gotten so far with a conversation that was as predictable and amusing as Quincy had imagined it would be, when he received a call from Daniel Malaterre, giving him an excuse to cut short the chat with his folks. He hoped that Justin Buckner had been taken into custody for one less headache for Giselle to have to deal with.

After accepting the video call, Quincy watched the FBI special agent in charge's strained face appear on the screen, indicating that it wasn't the news he sought, and asked him point blank, "What do you have for me...?"

"It's not good," Daniel said with an edge to his tone of voice, as he took a breath. "After digging through Justin Buckner's confiscated files, the Bureau has been able to ascertain that Buckner has been using an alias in his efforts to evade authorities."

"Which is...?" Quincy asked impatiently.

"He's been going by the name Jesse Teague—an identity Buckner stole from one of his clients, a forty-one-year-old investor who passed away from bone cancer earlier this year."

"*Jesse* Teague," Quincy voiced, emphasizing the first name, which happened to be the name of the suspect in the disappearance of Jacinta Cruz, along with more ominous possibilities. "The name definitely means something..."

As Quincy overcame the shock that Justin Buckner might have been using the moniker Jesse Teague to escape justice while hiding in plain view, Daniel said matter-of-factly, "I suspected it would. We've been able to backtrack his movements and establish that in using this fake identification of Jesse Teague, Buckner was able to book a flight a few weeks ago to Anchorage, Alaska. There's no record that he ever left the state by plane..."

"So he is here," Quincy muttered under his breath. Giselle's instincts about her ex-fiancé were right on target. And apparently his capabilities were as diabolical as she feared. Even worse, if that was possible. "A man who goes by the name Jesse is suspected in the abduction of a local documentary-film producer," he told Daniel. "And may have also committed at least one murder in

Alaska, if not more than that. I have reason to believe Jesse Teague is Buckner's alter ego."

"Wow." Daniel knitted his brows. "If what you suspect about the man is true, coupled with being wanted for a cold-case murder in Virginia, then we have ourselves a bona fide serial killer. Not to mention Buckner's serious financial crimes…"

"Yeah, he's a real piece of work." Quincy snorted as he contemplated the disturbing situation that was playing out in real time before his eyes.

"I wish we'd been able to connect the dots sooner."

"Me too." Quincy felt that was a huge understatement, considering what Buckner had put Giselle through, then and now.

"But we only know what we know when we know it," Daniel offered.

Quincy twisted his lips begrudgingly. "That's the difficult part about this," he griped. "Not being able to put the pieces together regarding a stalker and psychopath beforehand in order to stop him before so much damage could be done to Giselle and Buckner's other victims."

"Now that we do have the bead on the murder suspect possibly hiding out in your neck of the woods, we need to take him down—before he can do more harm," Daniel argued, narrowing his eyes. "Toward that end, the Bureau has already reached out to my special agent in charge counterpart with the Anchorage field office, Bonnie Rawlings, to assist you guys in the ABI in capturing the fugitive financial planner."

"Okay," Quincy said, welcoming any assistance in apprehending Justin Buckner to face justice.

"Beyond that, the FBI Norfolk field office, based

in Chesapeake, that's investigating Buckner's alleged white-collar crimes and the Chesapeake Police Department, after him for murder, have also been notified as players in the game."

"We're all on the same team here," Quincy stated. "With the same goal in mind."

"Yeah." Daniel titled his head. "Until Buckner's in custody, you might want to do whatever you need to do in protecting Giselle from her stalker."

Quincy nodded. "I intend to," he promised and ended the call. He immediately called Giselle, hating the thought that Buckner could be watching her at that very moment, fully intent on carrying out his threats. Or could the fugitive have cut his losses and left the state for parts unknown to try and save himself?

"Hey," Giselle said pleasantly when answering the phone.

At least she appears to be safe at the moment, Quincy told himself and then said equably, "Can you meet me at the Owl's Den when you get off work?"

"Of course." She paused. "What's up?"

"I'll tell you when you get there," he answered evasively, believing that it was best that they discuss this in person, while at the same time, putting together a plan to protect her from Buckner and his hostile intentions toward her.

"Uh, all right," she said simply, leaving it at that. "I'm off at five. See you shortly thereafter."

"Okay."

After ending that call, Quincy phoned Lieutenant Ron Valdez, his superior at the ABI Soldotna Major Crimes Unit, and apprised him of the alarming new twist in his investigation into the death of Sadie Pisano and disappearance of Jacinta Cruz. Quincy then called Sergeant Miriam Fontaine so the Taller's Creek PD was fully informed on where things stood in the cases that suddenly had Justin Buckner as the apparent common denominator.

THE MOMENT GISELLE entered the Owl's Den bar, she felt a chill in the air. Was it her imagination? Or was something going on that was about to rock her world over and beyond the strong presence of Quincy in her life?

She spotted him at the bar where Giselle had had cocktails with Jacinta before her friend had simply vanished without explanation or indication of where she was. With the search for her on the Pippen Trail suspended, more or less, Giselle could only wonder if reaching a dead end meant that Jacinta's disappearance would be swept under the rug. Or if this was something akin to the calm before the storm.

"Hey," Quincy greeted her, lifting from his stool.

"Hey." Giselle studied his undecipherable eyes tentatively as they both sat down.

"What would you like to drink?"

"A glass of white wine would be nice."

"White wine it is." He ordered this and a beer for himself from a slim thirtysomething female bartender with dark hair in a windswept bob.

After the drinks came, Giselle gazed at Quincy's face. Her first thought was that he had bad news to share about Jacinta. Had they found her—dead?

Cringing at the notion, Giselle asked uneasily, "So, why are we here...?" Instead of having drinks in a more intimate setting, such as her place or his. "What's happened?"

Quincy tasted his mug of beer first and then, regarding her squarely, responded, "Justin Buckner is very likely in Alaska—"

"What?" Her eyes widened. "He's here…?"

"Looks that way." Quincy's brow creased. "According to my FBI source, Buckner's been operating with a stolen identity." He sucked in a deep breath. "Jesse Teague."

Hey, met a new guy named Jesse. Cool to hang out with. Wish me luck!

As Jacinta's text replayed in her head, Giselle asked, "Are we talking about the same Jesse who may have kidnapped Jacinta—or worse…?"

"I think we have to assume that to be the case when you add it all up," Quincy told her lamentably. "Buckner stole the name from a dead client and was able to use his new identity to fly to Alaska from Virginia under the radar while covering his tracks in evading the authorities."

Giselle narrowed her eyes. "Are you saying that Justin's been here since…"

"He's apparently been stalking you in Taller's Creek for at least as long as you believed he was," Quincy told her straightforwardly.

"Unbelievable!" Her voice shook as Giselle mused about the warning bells that had been triggered from her earlier sightings of Justin, who was apparently intent on making good on his threats to psychologically victimize her as a prelude to coming after her directly.

Quincy drank more beer. "Buckner's menace goes much further than stalking you," he pointed out. "Not only is he the prime suspect in Jacinta Cruz's disappearance as Jesse, the last person she was seen with, but Buckner has to be considered a suspect in the murder of Sadie Pisano…and maybe others in your circle of friends—"

"What are you talking about?" Giselle demanded, taking a sip of the wine.

Quincy jutted his chin thoughtfully. "According to the coordinator for the search and rescue, a person who led them to Neve Chenoweth's body also matched the description of Jesse—suggesting that he may have known in advance where to find her."

Giselle peered at him. "Are you saying that Neve's death was no accident?"

He hedged, tasting the beer. "I'm saying it may need to be looked into further, along with Yuki Kotake's alleged suicide and, as I said, Sadie Pisano's death. Given that Buckner's been accused of murdering a woman in Virginia, among his other suspected offenses, it's really not too much of a stretch at this point to believe that as part of his warped fixation on you, Buckner may have killed more women…"

Giselle's shoulders slumped at the thought that she could have unknowingly, but still true nonetheless, been responsible for others losing their lives. How was she supposed to live with that? "I'm not sure what to say," she stammered sullenly. "Or what not to…"

"There's nothing for you to say that you haven't already said," Quincy told her. "None of what Buckner has done or may have done is your fault in any way, shape or form, to be clear. Bad things happen to good people all the time—no matter the dynamics that may have come into play—and it can't be prevented by trying to micromanage each and every aspect of our lives. It's not your job to read the mind of an unhinged, spiteful person you once knew. Whatever crimes Buckner has committed, it's all on him. Not you."

Giselle sipped the wine, acquiescing to this reality, no matter how much she wanted to take responsibility, after being on the run from Justin for three years and counting. "So, what now?" she wondered.

"We wait it out till Buckner's in custody. Now that the cat's out of the bag as to his likely whereabouts, law enforcement personnel from multiple jurisdictions are coming after him, hot and heavy," Quincy voiced sharply. "That old adage *He can run, but he can't hide* will bear out. Buckner will have to answer for any crimes he has committed."

"I sure hope so." Giselle sighed. "Not sure how much more of this—him—I can take, honestly."

Quincy touched her shoulder. "You won't have to take anything else he cares to dish out. But in the meantime, I'd like to stay at your place tonight—in case Buckner is stupid enough to show his face and come after you before we haul him off to jail."

Giselle nodded, placing her hand on his. "Yes, I'd like that," she told him. The thought of being alone and possibly forced to confront the man who had made her life so miserable three years ago was enough to make her nauseous. Having Quincy there to protect her and be the man she had come to depend on as a romantic partner and friend was more than she could hope for at this stage of her journey through life.

"Good." Quincy finished off his drink and rose. "Let's go."

"All right."

Sipping a bit more of the wine, Giselle gave him a brief smile, trying her best to block out for now what she'd just learned about her ex, and then stood to accompany Quincy to her apartment.

AFTER FOLLOWING HER HOME, still worried about Justin Buckner being on the loose, Quincy took some solace in the knowledge that they had the murder and kidnapping suspect at a disadvantage. Buckner had no idea that they had pinned down his likely whereabouts and were in full pursuit, no matter what his warped mind had planned for Giselle. As for Jacinta Cruz, Quincy could only hope that it wasn't too late to rescue her from wherever Buckner probably had her stashed away. That was assuming she hadn't already been disposed of by the creep and buried somewhere in the vast Alaska wilderness.

So long as no body has materialized, I can't assume Jacinta is dead, Quincy told himself as he pulled into the parking lot behind Giselle's Honda. But they needed to find her, one way or the other. That notwithstanding, his current focus was on making sure that Giselle—the woman he was planning a future with—wasn't the next person to disappear. If this was truly Buckner's end game, it was incumbent upon Quincy, the ABI, FBI, Taller's Creek PD and other law enforcement with a vested interest to make sure the wanted man failed to achieve his objectives and answered for everything he had done.

After exiting his vehicle, Quincy walked over to Giselle and held her hand supportively, both remaining silent. Welcoming the opportunity to spend the night with her any chance he got, his primary reason this time around was to act as a shield between her and Justin Buckner—now that it appeared that, as Jesse Teague, the stalker and murder suspect was intent on waging a vindictive campaign against Giselle that likely would end in her death.

When they got to the door of her apartment, Quincy could tell right away that something was off. There were clear signs of forced entry. Meaning that whoever broke in could very well still be inside. And dangerous.

"Wait here!" Quincy ordered as he released Giselle's hand and removed his duty weapon from inside a hip holster.

Her eyes widened with consternation. "Do you think it's Justin…?"

"There's only one way to find out." Quincy met her gaze. "If anything goes wrong in there, get the hell away from here!"

Giselle nodded reluctantly and uttered, "Please be careful—"

"I will," he promised and slowly pushed open the door, and stepped inside with his Glock 22 leading the way.

Ready to shoot anyone who caught his eye and was threatening, Quincy cautiously made his way through the apartment, checking every nook and cranny. He half expected to find the place ransacked, perhaps out of frustration that Giselle wasn't there for Buckner to abduct. Or finish off, once and for all.

Instead, there seemed little indication, beyond the front door being forced open, that anything was out of the ordinary in the neat way Giselle kept her residence. But where was Muffin? Had the intruder taken the kitten as a souvenir? Or as a warning to Giselle for what was to come?

When Quincy got to the bedroom, he saw the kitten in a corner. It was lying there unmoving, as if asleep. But the unnatural positioning concerned him. As did the half-filled bowl of water nearby that she had obviously drunk from. What was in it?

As he approached, Quincy heard a shuffling noise behind him and whipped around to find Giselle standing there.

She batted her eyes and explained, "When you didn't come out, I had to know that you were okay."

Even if he wished she had stayed outside and potentially out of harm's way, Quincy could hardly fault Giselle for considering his own safety. "I am," he said tonelessly, knowing that the intruder had come and gone and thereby was no longer a threat. "But I fear that isn't the case for—"

Before he could finish, Giselle had pushed past Quincy and raced toward her kitten, while screaming her name in panic mode, "Muffin!"

At that point, Quincy could only assume the worst. Her beloved little kitten was dead.

Chapter Fifteen

Giselle stood on pins and needles in the reception area at Soldotna Animal Hospital on Sterling Highway, where they had rushed Muffin as soon as they'd established that the kitten was still alive, though unconscious.

"She has to be okay," Giselle cried, believing that whatever had happened to the kitten—who had vomited and had diarrhea before passing out—was likely the result of something in the water she had drunk. It coincided with the intruder breaking into her apartment. She was all but certain that it had been her deranged ex, Justin, sending her a clear message: *First your acquaintances, then your kitten and finally I'm coming to get you*, Giselle envisioned Justin saying menacingly inside her head. "Muffin looked so fragile," she moaned.

Quincy pulled Giselle into his muscular arms comfortingly and said, "Let's just wait and see what the vet has to say, and hope for the best." He breathed warmly onto her cheek. "The fact that Muffin's alive and we were able to get her here has to be a good sign," he asserted.

"I hope you're right." Giselle sniffled and dried her tears on his shirt. "I just can't imagine my life without that adorable little one." At the same time, she did find herself imagining a life with Quincy, whom Giselle found herself growing closer to with each passing day. Even in the face of the danger that Justin posed to both of them as long as he remained on the loose in and around Taller's Creek.

"Then don't," Quincy told her insistently, "until it's been determined otherwise."

Just then, they saw the veterinarian enter the room, getting their attention. Giselle pulled away from Quincy and, with her heart pounding, asked the thirtysomething vet nervously, "What happened to my kitten?"

Doctor Lynette Suzuki—who was slender and wearing a white lab coat, with brunette hair in a midi flick cut—touched her square eyeglasses and responded reticently, "I hate to say this, but I'm afraid she was poisoned."

Giselle tried to come to terms with what she had strongly suspected already as Quincy asked, "What type of poison?"

"She ingested phorate, which is a pesticide that's usually found in organophosphorus insecticides," Lynette explained. "I'm guessing that this wasn't accidental—"

"Very unlikely," Quincy said flatly. "Pretty sure this was a deliberate act!"

"Sorry to hear that." The vet frowned. "Hope you figure out who's behind it…"

"I think we already have," he muttered with an edge to his inflection, glancing at Giselle and back before asking, "So, what's the prognosis?"

"Will Muffin live?" Giselle followed anxiously, eyeing the vet.

Lynette took a breath and then smiled. "Yes, your kitten will live. Fortunately it doesn't appear as though she ingested too much of it—as cats and kittens are sensitive to unusual tastes and are quick to reject them—but enough to cause her to vomit, have diarrhea and likely struggle to walk before eventually losing consciousness. This was potentially life threatening," she admitted, "had you not acted quickly in bringing her here..."

Giselle breathed in a huge sigh of relief. "So, Muffin will make a full recovery?"

"I don't see why not." Lynette flashed her teeth. "The anti-seizure medication we gave her, along with supplemental oxygen and IV fluids, have done their job in overcoming the poisoning. We'd like to keep Muffin for a day or two to monitor her recovery. After that, you should be able to take her home and give her all the loving attention she needs to be back to herself in no time."

"Thank you so much, Dr. Suzuki," Giselle gushed gratefully.

Lynette smiled. "Happy to do my part to get your cute little kitten up on her feet again."

"We'll be sure to do our part to make that happen," Quincy assured her, which warmed Giselle's heart in telling her that he was starting to truly see them as united in their relationship. Which included Muffin and Quincy's family.

On the way back to her apartment, Giselle looked at him from the passenger seat of his car as she considered the near miss with Muffin and Justin, the most likely perpetrator of the poisoning and still at large, and asked, ill at ease, "What now?"

Quincy turned her way and responded, "We grab some of your things and you stay at my house—where you'll be safe, and so will Muffin when she's released—till we can get Buckner in custody."

"All right." Giselle was not about to be defiant in any way in resisting Quincy's take-charge offer to provide her with the security of his home while Justin was gunning for her. "Is it possible that someone other than Justin broke into my apartment?" she had to ask, knowing that there had been some occasional burglaries in the area. Usually with local teens, looking for cash for drugs, as the culprits. Even in pondering this, Giselle wasn't about to give her vengeful ex-fiancé stalker the benefit of the doubt, knowing he was apparently in Alaska, operating as Jesse.

"Possible, yes—probable, no," Quincy told her, gazing over the steering wheel. "Buckner, fixated on you and still thinking he's kept you in the dark as to his presence, had the most to gain by poisoning Muffin and leaving you guessing…"

"Figured as much," Giselle admitted perceptively.

"With any luck, the Crime Scene Unit will find his prints or DNA inside your apartment." Quincy pulled into the lot. "Short of that, we still know that he's after you. Buckner isn't likely to stop his harassment—including possibly using Jacinta as bait, if she's still alive—in order to do what he's set out to do."

"Which is to punish me for daring to leave him," she uttered painfully.

"Yes, but I'm not about to allow that to happen," Quincy promised. "Whatever damage Buckner's already put into play, he won't hurt you directly, Giselle. Beyond what you've already experienced in your past involvement with the fugitive. Now, let's go get your things…"

She nodded and contemplated the lengths to which Justin had apparently already gone in following through on his promises, as Giselle wondered if she would still be able to win the battle against a determined foe before he could be arrested and put away for the rest of his miserable life.

GISELLE AGAIN ran for her life, sure that to do anything less would result in her demise. Justin was intent upon making sure she didn't have one more second to cherish, much less hours, days, weeks or years. So determined was he to have her at all costs as his to control like his personal sex slave and trophy wife. Or see to it that she paid a heavy price that there was simply no walking back from.

But it was a place that she was unwilling to go. Not by a long shot. He couldn't have her. No matter his wishes to the contrary. She deserved so much better in a man. In a husband. In a solid and sustainable relationship. In the great love of her life and times, and father of her children. Much more than a person so distasteful and obsessed with molding her into someone and something she wasn't. She would rather die a thousand times than succumb to his irrational demands. No matter the personal sacrifices she would have to make.

Sucking in a deep, ragged breath, Giselle ran up the quarter-turn staircase in the waterfront mansion to the second story, the determined attacker in hot pursuit like a man possessed. If she could just get to the primary suite and lock the door behind her, maybe she could survive the ordeal by phoning Quincy to come to her rescue. Only then could she ever hope to have a nor-

*mal life, with a normal and loving man to give her love
to in return.*

*Racing in her bare feet across the hardwood flooring
in the long hallway, Giselle nearly tripped but corrected
herself from falling. But even losing half a step shortened
the distance between her and the man who wanted her
dead, whatever it took. Still, she forged ahead, reaching the room she'd once shared with her stalker, but
seeing it now as nothing more than a prison for which
there was no escape.*

*Once inside, Giselle barely had a chance to take in
the expensive Italian furniture, some of which she had
chosen herself, while simultaneously attempting to slam
the door shut before he could stop her—when Justin was
able to do just that.*

*Using his superior strength, he forced the door open,
knocking her to the floor in the process. Scrambling to
her feet, she ran toward the king-size bed, hoping to
somehow get to the other side and maybe step onto the
balcony for some kind of escape. Instead, he caught up
to her, grabbed her by the hair and threw her down hard
onto the dark blue comforter.*

*Before Giselle could even breathe, Justin had climbed
on top of her, where he pulled the phorate poison out
of his pocket and forced it down her throat; then as she
was choking, he placed his large hands around her neck,
his face contorted with fury like a demon. She tried to
fight him off, to no avail, as she felt her strength fading
fast—along with whatever life she had left.*

*He was strangling and poisoning her to death. And
there was nothing she could do about it. Other than accept her fate. And pray that the end came quickly.*

Giselle looked into the evil eyes of death. Glaring back at her was Justin.

She tried to scratch his face, wipe the wicked grin of pleasure off it—but he kept just out of reach of her flailing hands and fingernails. Before she could breathe her last breath, Giselle managed to squeeze from her mouth that she detested him with a passion—to which he seemed to draw upon in his contorted face and sick satisfaction in achieving his ultimate objective of taking her life.

GISELLE SHRIEKED AS she sought to fight off her attacker. He seemed relentless in his determination to make her pay for depriving him of his desire to possess her.

A deep and familiar voice began to cut through the dense fog of sleep as she heard the gentle tone say, "Wake up, Giselle. It's only a dream—" Her eyelids flew open, and adjusting to the low light, she stared into the face of Quincy.

"Quincy…" Giselle's mouth was dry, but she had broken out into a cold sweat.

"I've got you," he said softly, cradling her protectively in his arms.

"Dream…?"

"Actually, a nightmare." He kissed the top of her head. "It's over. You're safe now," he promised.

"I feel safe—with you," Giselle told him as she wept. "Justin was trying to kill me with poison and his large hands," she said, taking a deep breath. "It seemed so real."

"It wasn't." Quincy held her closer. "Just some bad memories manifesting themselves in your head. I won't let him hurt you anymore," he promised, making Giselle believe every word as she clung to Quincy for the rest of the night.

QUINCY WAS UP bright and early the next morning, allowing Giselle to get some extra sleep after a restless night, while he made breakfast. He hated that Justin Buckner had succeeded on some level in getting under her skin through both dreams and his mere presence in Alaska. The sooner they could find the murder suspect and white-collar offender, the sooner Quincy could give Giselle back her sense of security, health and well-being.

He was standing over the electric griddle when Giselle walked into the kitchen. She looked sleepy eyed and was wearing one of his shirts while barefoot.

She said softly, "Good morning."

"Good morning." Quincy saw that her hair was a bit tangled from the pillow, but it was a turn-on nonetheless, like the rest of the package she presented.

"Just grabbed the first piece of clothing I could find," she claimed in explaining the shirt.

"No problem." He grinned. "The shirt looks much better on you than me," he assured her.

She colored self-consciously. "If you say so."

"Hungry?"

"I'm starving," she answered.

"Good." Quincy turned to the griddle and back. "I'm making omelets with shredded cheese, diced ham and sautéed bell peppers."

Giselle smiled. "Sounds delicious."

"Wait till you taste it," he bragged. "Made coffee. Help yourself."

"I will—thanks." She moved closer and met his eyes thoughtfully. "Look, about last night…"

Quincy held her gaze, cutting in to say, "No explanation necessary. After what you were slammed with yesterday…it was a lot to absorb for anyone given the same dynamics—it's quite understandable that it would seep into your dreams as a nightmare."

"Thanks for helping me get through it," she murmured tenderly.

"I was happy to come to your aid—and will gladly do so anytime I'm around." If he had a serious say in the matter, Quincy wanted that to be often. "Time to eat," he told her and flipped her omelet onto a plate.

A few minutes later, they were sitting on a sofa bench at the midcentury-modern wooden table in the eating nook having breakfast when Giselle grimaced and said thoughtfully, "Do you think that Justin has Jacinta? Or is she…?"

"We'll keep hope alive—and Jacinta too," Quincy responded calmly, "until there's solid proof that she's a victim of foul play. In the meantime, we're doing everything we can to find her."

"Okay." Giselle lifted her coffee mug and took a sip contemplatively.

Quincy waited a beat and then threw out casually, but in all seriousness, after tasting his own coffee, "I was thinking that maybe you should take off work for a day or two—till we can locate and bring in Buckner. If he did break into your apartment, besides knowing where you live—he likely also knows you work at Taller's Creek Books and could come after you there…"

"I was thinking the same thing," Giselle responded

without hesitation while eating. "Since chances are that it was Justin who sent the orange roses after all, there's no reason to tempt fate. Or put the lives of my colleagues at the bookstore in any further jeopardy."

Quincy nodded, in complete agreement. "Exactly." He sliced a fork into his omelet. "Beyond that, although I have a good security system, to be on the safe side, I'll arrange with the Taller's Creek Police Department to have patrols in this area to keep an eye out for Buckner and any signs of trouble…"

"Good idea." She offered him a tepid smile. "I appreciate everything you've done for me."

"Haven't really done much," he argued, downplaying it. "But I hope to have the opportunity to give you everything you deserve in life."

Her eyes grew. "Seriously?"

"Yeah, seriously." Quincy saw no reason to pull back from the way he felt about her and wanting this to become more of a permanent thing. "We have something really good here, and I want to keep it going."

Giselle gazed at him. "Me too," she uttered in earnest and paused. "Once Justin is finally out of the picture for good, we can definitely work on that."

Quincy nodded in full agreement and started to imagine just what their lives could be like together—once the bogeyman had been removed from the equation once and for all.

Chapter Sixteen

On Monday, Quincy huddled with the ABI's Major Crimes Unit in Soldotna, along with FBI officials and law enforcement from Taller's Creek and Chesapeake, as they assessed the situation in the search for wanted fugitive and murder suspect Justin Buckner and as yet still missing and presumed to have been abducted Jacinta Cruz.

In Quincy's mind, Justin—masquerading as his late client Jesse Teague—almost certainly was still holding Jacinta somewhere in the Kenai Peninsula Borough, as a thorough search for the documentary-film producer had come up empty. There was no evidence to indicate whether she was dead or alive, much less being held against her will, though this was in all likelihood probably the case.

But this doesn't mean Buckner hasn't killed and buried her—or left her to die, Quincy thought realistically as he stood in front of the conference room and considered the case against Justin Buckner that was growing stronger as the evidence started to come in.

That included DNA that had been collected from Giselle's apartment. When entered into the FBI's CODIS database, the DNA profile matched that of Justin Buckner's on file, indicating that, at the very least, he had been inside her place (putting him in Taller's Creek in and of itself) and almost certainly was responsible for poisoning Muffin.

Just as damning was a fingerprint found by the Crime Scene Unit at the residence of Yuki Kotake. The Bureau's Integrated Automated Fingerprint Identification System got a hit on it, identifying the print as belonging to Buckner—leaving no doubt that he had been at her cabin at some point and could have made it appear as though Yuki had taken her own life with a firearm. Moreover, the toxicology test on Yuki surprisingly had found no drugs or alcohol in her system, which was inconsistent to Quincy, given her history of depression and using antidepressants as a means to control it—both of which were common correlates in cases of suicide. This called into question whether or not her death had been self-inflicted or cold-blooded murder by someone with an axe to grind.

Likewise, Sadie Pisano's drugging and murder, as someone who'd worked at the same bookstore as Giselle, with the orange roses sent there by an anonymous person, might have been a tip-off or forerunner to Sadie's death when the events were broken down. Quincy felt this had Buckner's fingerprints written all over it with what he now knew about the fixated and atrocious ex of Giselle.

Then there'd been someone fitting the suspect's description seen at both the Pippen Trail, where Neve Chenoweth had supposedly died accidentally, and at her candlelight vigil. Quincy would bet a month's salary that they were one and the same person: Justin Buckner.

And that, all things considered, Neve's death might not have been an accident as they'd first thought.

Quincy told the group bluntly, "There's every reason to believe that Justin Buckner, using the alias Jesse Teague, is not only in Alaska right now but has very likely perpetrated a number of serious offenses in the state while evading authorities elsewhere—including at least one murder, if not more, and the kidnapping of Jacinta Cruz. Along with poisoning a precious little kitten that belongs to Giselle Kinard, the object of Buckner's misguided and unhinged affections," Quincy had to say, knowing just how beloved Muffin was by Giselle, whom she was back with now, nursing the kitten to full health. His brows drew together as he said pointedly, "I think it's safe to say that Buckner has to be considered armed and extremely dangerous—and needs to be located fast and taken into custody, as he's clearly a loose and somewhat unpredictable cannon."

Lieutenant Ron Valdez chimed in, standing beside him and stating, "I've directed Alaska State Troopers to work hand in hand with other law enforcement to track down the fugitive. Buckner has a lot of places he can hide in our vast and circuitous wilderness, but we have a much better grip on our neck of the woods than he does. That gives us an advantage that he can't hope to match as he tries to evade the law while committing other crimes in Alaska." Valdez wrinkled his brow. "Trying to get to the missing Jacinta Cruz before it's too late is of the utmost importance if we're to find her still alive. We know what Buckner is capable of as a murder suspect in both Alaska and Virginia. As Quincy Lankard has pointed out, time is of the essence in Buckner's capture."

To add to the arrows pointing at the suspect, Sergeant Miriam Fontaine revealed that surveillance video obtained from a neighbor of Sadie Pisano's at Creeklin Apartments showed someone who fit Justin Buckner's current description running away from the building the day the Kenai Peninsula College student had been killed.

When Quincy put this together with other Buckner sightings relative to Giselle's environment, along with more than enough other direct and circumstantial evidence, it seemed to all but clinch that they had the right suspect in their crosshairs in the bathtub murder of Sadie. Which then tied in with other criminal behavior alleged by the suspect in and around Taller's Creek. That included the stalking of Giselle, with the targeting of Muffin a clear reflection of that.

FBI Anchorage Special Agent Leigh McCormick weighed in on the investigation. The thirtysomething, slender African American woman with a raven midlength Afro parted in the middle said authoritatively, "Based on what we have to work with, Justin Buckner, aka Jesse Teague, is not only a wanted white-collar offender— he has morphed into a serial killer. He's suspected in the cold-case homicide of Jenna Sweeney and the much more recent murder of Sadie Pisano, at the very least." Leigh gave a sigh. "Apparently Buckner's homicidal and predatory tendencies are fueled, in part, by a pathological desire to control those he's obsessed with. Such as the case of Ms. Sweeney and, apparently, his long-term obsession with Giselle Kinard—and the retaliatory violence to follow. Some of those targeted by the suspect are most likely incidental victims, as a calculated means to an end. Such as the apparent abduction of Jacinta Cruz.

Unless she's found soon, we can only assume that Buckner will want to dispose of her as a hindrance so that he can refocus on the one he's really after—"

Giselle, Quincy told himself before the pretty special agent could finish her insightful and ominous thoughts. It caused the hairs to rise on the back of his neck, aware that with each passing moment that Buckner remained on the loose, he posed a greater danger to Giselle. Though knowing she was safe at his house—with police keeping an eye on the property and otherwise patrolling the greater area—gave Quincy some comfort, it was hardly enough to want to take his foot off the gas. Not until the threat the murder suspect presented was completely eliminated.

GISELLE SAT ON a cushioned barnwood sectional in the great room playing with Muffin, who was pretty much back to herself, thankfully. The fact that Quincy had welcomed them into his house made things even better. She loved being there and felt right at home, imagining that was the case. Apparently Muffin did as well, as she flew out of Giselle's arms and scurried across the floor and out of sight.

Now, if only Jacinta can be found unharmed and Justin apprehended, it will put my mind at ease on that major front, Giselle told herself as she grabbed her mug of black coffee from the end table and took a sip. She figured that with the authorities hot on his trail, it wouldn't be long before his days of hurting others were over. Then she could breathe again and see just what her life might be like without the specter of her ex looming in the shadows.

When her cell phone rang, Giselle saw that the caller

was Ellen Ebsen. She wondered if there was a problem at the bookstore. Or maybe another delivery of orange roses.

"Hey," Giselle answered hesitantly.

"Hey," Ellen said. "I was trying to find a book that appears to be misplaced and hoped you could help."

"I can try…"

After a moment or two, Ellen uttered, "Actually, I just wanted to check on you."

"Really?" Giselle pushed the phone closer to her ear.

"Yeah. With all this business about a killer at large— someone from your past—we all wanted to know that you're okay, along with your kitten…"

"We're both fine," Giselle promised, still feeling guilty that she had inadvertently brought Justin and his unwanted drama into all of their lives. "Wish I could be there, but with everything that's happened—"

"No one's blaming you for being stalked by a crazy ex-boyfriend," Ellen insisted. "Many of us have been down that road in one form or another—sometimes with tragic results. Thank goodness your situation is currently being dealt with appropriately by the authorities."

"I agree," Giselle told her, "and I appreciate the support."

"Hope to see you back at work soon," she said.

"You will."

Even as she said this, Giselle could only wonder if this was a sign that she needed to get back to what she loved most as a dancer. She hung up and took another sip of the coffee, pondering her life up to this point and where she needed to go from here—and who with.

AFTER PINGS FROM Jacinta's cell phone showed that her last call had been made by a cell tower in the Kenai Peninsula Borough, around Angler Drive, near Kenai Spur Highway, the ABI and other law enforcement agencies put their focus on the wooded area that had a number of farmhouses spread out amid the western hemlock and white spruce trees.

Quincy drove his Ford Police Interceptor Utility SUV into the borough with fellow ABI investigator Alan Edmonston in the passenger seat, hoping to catch a break in trying to locate the missing documentary-film producer.

Beyond that, Quincy needed to put an end to Justin Buckner's reign of terror in Alaska—much of which appeared to be driven by a personal vendetta against Giselle—and elsewhere. But first they had to pinpoint exactly where the fugitive's base of operation was in a region that, even when narrowed in scope, still left Buckner with breathing room to lay low.

"Sorry that Giselle Kinard has been swept up in the entanglement with Buckner," Alan remarked, breaking the silence between them.

"Me too," Quincy said regretfully. He had mentioned earlier that they were involved. "She wanted nothing to do with him—but evidently he didn't seem to get the message. Or actually, Buckner got it loud and clear but chose to reject it like others unnaturally fixated on someone they couldn't possess."

"She did the right thing to get away from Buckner," Alan said supportively. "The fact that he wouldn't leave well enough alone and has come after her doesn't change that."

"True." Quincy stared through the windshield. "We just need to get to him first."

"Yeah." Alan took a breath. "So, is it serious between you two?"

Not needing to even think about the question, Quincy was able to answer straightforwardly, "Yes, it's serious." That was certainly the case from his perspective. He was sure that Giselle felt the same way.

"Glad to hear that. I know I talked about not rushing things, but when you know, you know," he argued, "and you just have to jump in with both feet like I did so many years ago and am better for it."

"That you are." Quincy grinned at him and felt the pressure of hoping to measure up to a lifetime of wedded bliss. He felt more than up to the challenge should he and Giselle manage to get there. "We'll see how it goes." Once they no longer had the albatross of Justin Buckner weighing them down like an anchor.

The conversation was cut short when a call came in from Lieutenant Valdez, informing them that a small DPS drone had managed to cut through the trees and spot an orange Toyota 4Runner behind a farmhouse on Angler Drive. A run on the license plate showed that it was registered to Jacinta Cruz.

"We discovered that the farmhouse itself is owned by a Harold Tanoue," Valdez said over the speakerphone. "He's been renting out the place to—you guessed it—Jesse Teague, Justin Buckner's stolen moniker. There's no outward sign on the property of Buckner or his presumed abductee, Ms. Cruz, but we can't get a good fix on the interior of the residence," the lieutenant said. "We've got a SWAT team, Special Emergency Reaction Team, K-9 unit and personnel from the Alaska Fugitive Task Force en route."

Believing that Buckner and Jacinta could well be holed up inside the farmhouse, with her life hanging in the balance, Quincy got the address, then told him, "We'll meet them there." He headed that way, putting on the speed, knowing there were no seconds to spare.

After arriving at the location, Quincy parked just out of view from the farmhouse while surveying the place through binoculars. There were blinds on the windows, effectively keeping anyone from seeing inside.

"What do you think?" Alan asked. "They in there?"

"Maybe." Quincy eyed the property and saw, as the drone's aerial surveillance had indicated, no other vehicle besides Jacinta's 4Runner. It led him to believe that, given the location, Buckner would most likely need his own vehicle to get around in. "Or maybe not," he told the trooper. "Let's check it out."

"Shouldn't we wait for backup?"

"Probably," Quincy reasoned but rejected this. "If Buckner is inside, catching him off guard might be the better way to go. Especially if we can rescue his captive at the same time."

Alan contemplated this for a long moment before relenting. "Okay, let's do it."

They left the SUV wearing ballistic vests, removed their Glock 22s from holsters and slowly made their way into the woods and approached the farmhouse. Hearing only the sounds of red-flanked bluetail birds chirping overhead, Quincy signaled to Alan to go around the back, while he would charge in the front door.

Nodding, Alan separated from him, and Quincy gave him time to get in place before moving quickly himself toward the house. Feeling it was now or never, he chose *now* and quietly turned the doorknob of the wooden door, and it opened.

As he was moving inside, ready to confront the suspect, instead Quincy saw Alan rush in from the rear. At first glance, they saw nothing unusual in the sparsely furnished open-concept interior space with worn hardwood flooring.

It was only after he'd made his way to the primary bedroom that Quincy homed in on the female lying on the floor next to an unmade wooden farmhouse bed. He recognized the slender, blond-haired Hispanic woman as Jacinta Cruz. She was naked and surrounded by her own blood. Several puncture marks on her body told him that she had been stabbed. As did the defensive wounds on the victim's arms.

Rushing to her as he called out to Alan, Quincy felt for a pulse in Jacinta's neck and realized that, though seriously injured and unconscious, the documentary filmmaker and Giselle's friend was still alive.

"Call 911!" he ordered as Alan stepped into the room.

As they hoped to save Jacinta's life—while other law enforcement personnel arrived at the house in full force—her presumed attacker, Justin Buckner, was nowhere to be found, giving Quincy more reason for concern.

JUSTIN WATCHED FURTIVELY from the woods as a patrol car drove by the trooper's house where Giselle was hiding out. He had sent her a message when poisoning her kitten, knowing it would freak her out. Also, this made it clear that he could get to her whenever or wherever he wanted. Even though he doubted she was aware that it was her ex-fiancé who was behind the kitten crisis. Or, for that matter, the ordeals he'd put some others in her new life through.

That included Jacinta Cruz, whom he'd stabbed and left to die.

Not to mention what he'd done to Neve Chenoweth.

Yuki Kotake.

Sadie Pisano.

And all right under Giselle's dainty little nose.

It was merely a prelude of what Justin knew he wanted to do to her—his ex-fiancée who had dared to walk out on him and the relationship in marriage that Giselle had promised him.

Soon, very soon, she would experience in real time the same thing that Jenna Sweeney had made him to do her.

Only then would he be free at last of the rage that had built up inside him like volcanic gases, that powered this need—in fact, requirement—for an eruption of revenge against the one who had betrayed him.

Justin sucked in a deep breath and thought briefly about needing to escape Alaska afterward, with the feds and others intent upon taking him down. He hoped to stay a few steps ahead of them at every turn. Something he had done well his entire life, to one extent or another.

But at the moment, it was Giselle whom he was most focused on. He couldn't wait to see the frightened expression on her lovely face when they were eye to eye. And she was, once again, under his control.

Before he made sure her life had been cut much shorter than she ever envisioned, once upon a time.

Justin regarded the house once more, imagining what Giselle might be doing inside and wishing he were there with her right now, before forcing himself to vacate the scene as another patrol car approached as a deterrence.

Only for the time being.

Chapter Seventeen

Giselle rushed in her car to Central Peninsula Hospital after learning from Quincy that Jacinta had been airlifted there, in serious condition after being stabbed—and was in the emergency department, fighting for her life. The fact that they had found her friend alive at all was, to Giselle, a true miracle, given Jacinta's apparent abduction by Justin posing as Jesse—and his established penchant for harming women who came into his crosshairs.

But that didn't quell her feeling of being ill at ease for what Jacinta had been put through by him as she tried to come out on the other end in surviving. Or the knowledge that Justin had managed to evade capture and was, as such, still on the loose.

He couldn't have gotten very far, Giselle told herself as she reached the hospital. Surely the authorities had to be closing in on him to take him into custody before Justin was able to inflict more damage on those he chose to.

She parked and raced inside the hospital.

Quincy greeted Giselle in the lobby of the emergency department. "Hey," he muttered lowly, giving her a quick hug.

She gazed up at him and asked diffidently, "Any word on Jacinta's condition?"

"Not yet." He frowned beneath his campaign hat. "She's still in surgery."

Giselle's eyes watered. "I can't believe Justin did this to her…" In reality, she knew exactly what he was capable of—forcing her to run away from him as far as she could get. Only for him to track her down and go after people she knew. She wiped her eyes. "He can't get away with this."

"He won't," promised Quincy in a stern tone of voice. "We're scouring the borough for the black Kia Telluride we believe Buckner is driving, as well as any sign of the fugitive. It's only a matter of time before this ends—one way or another."

"I'll believe it when I see it," Giselle muttered with misgivings—fearful that based on his unsettling history of eluding the authorities, Justin would find some way, somehow, to escape the dragnet for his capture. But she also knew how determined Quincy was to bring him in and let the various jurisdictions fight each other for justice in the multiple allegations against Justin. Her tone was softer when Giselle uttered confidently, "I know you'll get him."

Quincy nodded understandingly and looked over her shoulder. "Your friends are here," he said evenly.

Giselle turned to see Seth, Kimberly, Ethan, Pablo and some other friends of Jacinta. All looked terribly distressed, and it made Giselle want to cry again. She embraced them in a group hug, and they all waited with bated breath to learn the fate of the documentary filmmaker.

When the surgeon came into the waiting room, Giselle

found herself clutching Quincy's muscular arm in anticipation of the news on Jacinta.

"I'm Doctor Peggy Itamura," she said equably.

Giselle met the large brown eyes of the doctor in her late thirties, who was small boned beneath bloodied scrubs and had black hair in a razor cut, and asked her what everyone wanted to know, "Is Jacinta going to pull through?"

Dr. Itamura sighed and answered evasively, "Ms. Cruz was stabbed multiple times and sustained some serious injuries, including a collapsed lung, along with losing a lot of blood. The surgery went well—better than expected—but it's still touch and go at this point." She took a breath. "The next twenty-four hours will be crucial for her survival. If all goes well, she stands a good chance to make a full recovery. Let's keep our fingers crossed..."

"Definitely," Giselle assured her, feeling this was the best any of them could have hoped for, given the grave manner in which Justin left Jacinta to die. Knowing her friend was a fighter, Giselle had to trust she could overcome this serious brush with death—refusing to believe otherwise. Giselle gazed at the doctor and asked, "When can we see her?"

"It'll be a while," she replied. "Ms. Cruz is still in the recovery room and will later be moved to the ICU, where visitation is mostly limited to family members, as she begins the recovery process, so I suggest you all go home for now. You can come back tomorrow—or call—to check on her."

"Okay," Kimberly said acceptingly, and others were quick to agree.

That included Giselle, who certainly didn't want to impede upon Jacinta getting through this crucial period in her survival. "Will do," she concurred.

As the doctor walked away, Pablo said somberly, "I could use a drink. I'm headed over to the Owl's Den. Anyone care to join me…?"

Everyone was in agreement, except for Giselle and Quincy, who was still on duty. For her part, she had little interest in getting drunk. Or socializing right now. Not till Jacinta was totally out of the woods.

"I'm just going to head home," Giselle told the group politely. She raised her eyes to meet Quincy's, knowing that her temporary residence was his house and had proven to be a good fit. "See you when I see you," she said.

As they began to disperse, Quincy held her elbow and asked, "Are you going to be okay?"

"Yeah." Giselle gave a nod, feeling she needed to be as strong as Jacinta surely had been when she'd undoubtedly gotten roped in by Justin as Jesse—only to live and possibly die to regret it.

"All right." He lowered his chin. "This will be over soon," he asserted.

"I sure hope so" was all she could say to that.

When his cell phone rang, Quincy said, "I need to get this."

Giselle waited and listened to his vague acknowledgments and responses before disconnecting. She watched his face harden while asking him, "What's happening?"

"Buckner was spotted lurking outside the hospital," Quincy told her. "We may have him cornered."

"That's great to hear." Though she wasn't getting her hopes up just yet, Giselle was guardedly optimistic that the nightmare could soon be coming to an end. "Go get him," she uttered, knowing that Quincy was eager to be there to slap the cuffs on Justin for his misdeeds under Quincy's jurisdiction.

"All right." He rested a hand on her shoulder. "I'll let you know how it turns out as soon as I have anything. In the meantime, I suggest you head straight to the house— and stay there till we have Buckner in custody."

"I'll do that," Giselle promised, then lifted her chin and gave him a quick kiss on the mouth. Both for good luck and because it felt good to express how strongly she felt about him and how she interpreted he felt about her.

Quincy smiled at her, touching his mouth in appreciation before running off. She headed in the opposite direction to hit the road herself.

TURNING ONTO NORTH BINKLEY STREET, where the suspect had been seen running toward, Quincy sped in his Ford Police Interceptor vehicle in that direction. Though he hated to leave Giselle at a time when her friend's life was still hanging in the balance, he was sure she understood, considering the sense of urgency he felt to nail Justin Buckner. In this instance, Quincy knew that he and Giselle were on the same page in wanting to end her misery once and for all, with Buckner being taken off the streets. There would be plenty of time afterward to chart a course for their own future. One which he was growing increasingly comfortable with insofar as wanting it to be a lasting one, with all the bells and whistles.

But right now, there was suspected killer and financial crimes offender Justin Buckner to deal with. His prints were all over the farmhouse where Jacinta Cruz had been discovered near death, leaving no doubt that Buckner was indeed his alter ego Jesse Teague and the culprit in Jacinta's kidnapping and violent victimization. To say nothing of his other suspected killings and white-collar crimes. The knife used against Jacinta had yet to be found but would inevitably tie the wanted fugitive to the crime.

Quincy couldn't help but wonder if, in showing up near the hospital, Buckner had actually been hoping to somehow reach Jacinta and finish the job of killing her. If that had been his intention, before apparently aborting the idea, it would have failed miserably. A guard had been posted at Jacinta's door as the victim of an attempted murder, to protect her from that point on.

When Quincy reached the destination—a small family-owned restaurant called Tulip's Dining and Desserts— where Buckner had last been spotted, police officers, state troopers, AST and FBI SWAT members and a Special Emergency Reaction Team had surrounded the North Binkley Street restaurant after safely evacuating employees and customers.

"Where is he?" Quincy asked Alan Edmonston regarding Buckner.

"The suspect ran through the restaurant and out the back door, where we have him trapped," Alan answered. "Just waiting for the word to flush him out."

Quincy spoke with Trooper Dave Norcross, who headed the SERT. "We need to get this done," he urged him, not wanting to risk the safety of the greater community by allowing the suspect to remain at large a moment longer.

Norcross, in his forties and brawny with gray hair in a buzz cut, agreed. "Let's go get him…"

Assuming that Buckner was armed and, obviously,

dangerous, the teams went in wearing body armor and body cameras and were able to apprehend the suspect without incident, as he cowered behind a dumpster.

It was only when he'd been escorted outside to the front of the restaurant while cuffed with zip ties that Quincy took a good look at the suspect. He was in his midtwenties, lean, short and bald-headed with brown eyes, wearing a dirty T-shirt, jeans and tennis shoes.

After identifying himself as being with the ABI, Quincy frowned as he asked the man straight on, "What's your name?"

"Larry Purnell," he muttered out of the corner of his mouth, while wreaking of alcohol mixed with cigarette stench.

Whether he was being straight or not, Quincy had no doubt that the man wasn't Justin Buckner, who was older, taller and had blue eyes. It was a case of mistaken identity. So where the hell was Justin Buckner?

Before digging deeper into that, Quincy got word that Buckner's black Kia Telluride, which they had issued a BOLO alert for, had been spotted on Unkeley Street, headed south.

Feeling his heart skip a beat, Quincy muttered an expletive under his breath as he realized that Giselle's longtime tormentor and multiple-murder suspect was headed right in the direction of his own house, where Giselle currently was—putting her in grave danger.

GISELLE JOGGED THROUGH the woods that consisted of balsam poplar and paper birch trees on Quincy's property. She welcomed the respite of her favorite pastime to both relieve the stress of recent happenings as well as the not-so-recent ones. She would continue maintaining fitness to keep up with Quincy and to hold her good looks well into the future, if she had her way.

She gazed through the trees and saw some harlequin ducks on the river. Giselle thought with a smile about how attached she had become to Alaska and all it had to offer, including a very good-looking and sexy state trooper. Now Justin was trying to ruin all that by pulling her back into his deranged past and a nonexistent future, were he to have his way.

At that moment, Giselle heard a slight rustling of the trees behind her. Instinctively she dug into the pocket of her blue fleece joggers, worn with a black crewneck tank and running shoes, and felt the pepper spray inside. Looking over her shoulder, she saw a couple of wood frogs chasing each other across the dirt—but no other human beings or, for that matter, wildlife to have to contend with.

Relaxing with a measured breath, Giselle realized that there was no reason, per se, to fear being attacked by her ex-fiancé in particular, whom she assumed had probably been captured by now—or was on the verge of it—on the other side of town after being cornered by the authorities. Other than that, she felt relatively safe on her runs in this part of Soldotna.

Hopefully by the time I get back to the house, Quincy will call to share the good news that Justin has been taken into custody, Giselle told herself as she headed back through the woods.

Just as she reached the house, Giselle received a text message from Quincy. She stepped inside, sure he was about to put her mind at ease, once and for all. But then she read the text.

Buckner still on loose. His SUV was seen near my place. May be coming after you. Lock the doors. On my way.

For an instant, Giselle froze as she read the terrifying words again and had to come to terms with the reality that Justin had not been captured. And worse, he could know where she was hiding from him.

She managed to regain her equilibrium and texted him back with simply Okay. Then she quickly locked the doors before pressing the stay button and entering the user code for the security system. Gazing out the picture windows in the great room, she saw no movement of anyone outside the house, suggesting he might not be out there planning to break in and attack her.

I have to stay strong, Giselle mused and believed that this was a battle Justin would not win in either his revenge against her or remaining at large to go after whomever he pleased.

Only then did Giselle think about Muffin, realizing that the kitten hadn't run up to her the moment she'd stepped inside the house—seemingly desperate for even more attention since being released from the vet.

"Where are you, Muffin?" Giselle asked, getting no kitten response, as she began to walk through the downstairs.

Seeing no sign of her, Giselle headed up the stairs. On the second floor, approaching one of the bedrooms, a muted meow sound came from one of the bedrooms other than the primary bedroom.

When she went inside, Giselle's heart thumped and her eyes sharpened as she saw Justin standing there in the flesh, holding Muffin in his arms.

"Guess cats—and kittens, too—really do have nine lives," Justin said with a snide laugh. Muffin belligerently scratched his hand, and he tossed the kitten to the floor and peered menacingly at Giselle. "Took me long enough, but I finally caught up to you—and fully intend to carry out exactly what I promised were you to ever leave me…"

Chapter Eighteen

Sergeant Miriam Fontaine was well aware that the hunt was on for the wanted fugitive Justin Buckner, whose identity theft had him operating as Jesse Teague. The suspected serial killer who had fled Virginia and a host of financial crimes to wreak havoc in Southcentral Alaska—or, more specifically, her own jurisdiction of Taller's Creek and adjacent Soldotna—angered Miriam to no end. As it would for any crimes of violence against local women and their alleged perpetrator.

That anger, though, did not extend to Giselle Kinard. Last Miriam knew, it was not a crime to relocate to the Last Frontier, as Alaska was known by people everywhere. Even if to escape an obsessed predator—who had apparently pulled out all the stops to pursue her, at risk to his capture. Or death. In Miriam's mind, this made Buckner all the more perilously uncontrollable, and he needed to be stopped at all costs.

When she spotted the black Kia Telluride SUV parked on the side of the road on Pamaner Street, Miriam pulled up behind it in her Ford Explorer Police Interceptor. She checked the license plate to verify her suspicions.

As expected from the BOLO alert, the SUV was the

vehicle Buckner was renting as Jesse Teague. After calling for backup, Miriam exited her police car. She immediately whipped out her Glock 22 duty pistol and approached the Kia Telluride.

A cursory glance inside showed that there were a couple of empty beer cans on the back seat, along with a pair of jeans and a dark hooded rain-resistant jacket.

But no Justin Buckner.

Miriam cast her eyes at the heavily wooded area nearby, believing that the suspect had fled into the trees. Or was there a method to his madness?

It occurred to her that Giselle Kinard, as the object of Buckner's fixation, had been given refuge at Quincy Lankard's private residence on Keystone Lane. Which was within reach from where Miriam stood.

She raced back to her vehicle and phoned this in before heading that way, while being informed that Quincy and other law enforcement were already en route and as eager as she was to prevent any further tragedy.

As MUFFIN SCURRIED nervously out of the room in Giselle's periphery, she found herself just staring squeamishly at her tormentor. He had shaven his full head of hair and added a five o'clock shadow to his face, which had become a little more weathered over the years. But the deep blue eyes were just as hardened, glaring back at her. Justin seemed every bit the physical specimen Giselle remembered, wearing an open gray soft-shell jacket over a rust-colored twill camp shirt, black jeans and dark gym shoes. She noted the knife tucked inside his waistband and blood on his hand from Muffin scratching it.

Stilling her nerves, Giselle asked him straightfor-wardly, as she considered the security system on the prem-ises that should have been activated with a break-in, "How did you get in here?"

Sporting a crooked grin on his lips, Justin answered, pleased with himself, "Oh, I have my ways. I've learned a trick or two about deactivating security systems, long enough to get in and out, when I need to."

I can't believe he outsmarted the security mecha-nisms, Giselle griped to herself. She was certain that Quincy had been notified of any break in the surveil-lance and was very likely en route to his house. But would he be too late to save her? Or could she find a way out of this herself—perhaps making a run for it—short of dying from trying?

Justin broke through her thoughts as he said with a laugh, "Have to admit, Giselle, you were a hard person to track down. Had me going from one state to the next, wondering where the hell you were hiding and how you managed to go underground without a trace. Frankly, I nearly gave up trying—believing you had successfully outmaneuvered me with your disappearing act. But I couldn't do that. Not when I had a score to settle with you—and wasn't about to let you off the hook. Never expected this to come to a head in Alaska of all places." He stopped abruptly as her cell phone rang, locking eyes with Giselle. "I wouldn't answer that if I were you," he threatened her.

She resisted the urge to ignore him and warn Quincy, whom Giselle was certain was the caller, letting the phone ring before it finally stopped. Ticking off Justin right now, she reasoned, while he had a knife, probably wasn't a smart idea. She had to trust that Quincy and his colleagues were privy to her current predicament and that help was on the way.

If only she could stay alive till then.

Giselle cast her eyes at Justin acrimoniously. "Why couldn't you just let me go, Justin—or should I say Jesse—and move on with your life?"

He chuckled in hearing the moniker. "Guess you would've figured it out sooner or later. I needed a new name to stay under the radar for as long as possible." His brows joined hostilely. "As for the other part—it's because we were meant to be together, Giselle," he insisted pointedly. "You agreed to marry me, and I wasn't going to allow you to renege on a promise. No way! Not when I gave you my heart—before you stomped on it..." He took his angry eyes off her for an instant and reached down on the side of the rustic guest bed and lifted up a dozen orange roses. "These are for you," he said coldly, handing them to her. "Like old times. Somehow it seemed fitting."

Giselle pretended to welcome the roses, putting the flowers to her nose but despising them and the man himself under the circumstances. "You sent the orange roses to the bookstore," she stated knowingly rather than asked.

"Yeah, it was me," Justin admitted. "It was meant to play with your head for a bit—to make things interesting— till the time came to meet up face-to-face."

Narrowing her eyes contemptuously, Giselle threw the roses onto the floor and blared with all but certainty, "Why did you have to go after Sadie? As well as Neve, Yuki and Jacinta, who's now clinging to her life...?"

"Because they were a means to an end," Justin replied heartlessly while confessing to his role. "I warned you what would happen if you ever left me. And I'm a man of my word, if nothing else. I wanted you to feel the pain through these other women you were connected with. Slowly but surely. Till it was your turn. Anything less, and it wouldn't have hit home what a huge disappointment you turned out to be—and just what it would cost you. Staging the deaths as accidental, suicide, random or whatever was easy and only to throw off the authorities—and you... Other than that, they meant nothing to me. Not really. Not even close to the pleasure I'll get when I make sure you—just like Jenna, the last woman I foolishly chose to love, who betrayed me too and had to die as a result—breathe your last breath!"

Justin whipped out the knife, which had a serrated blade that was at least eight inches long, and Giselle found herself backing up to the picture window with the vertical blinds closed. Her pulse racing as he moved toward her and put the knife up to her throat, she risked instant death by stating the obvious, "You won't get away with this, Justin!"

"Watch me." He laughed overconfidently, while effectively cutting off any means for escape. "You see, I've got a plan. I'll take off in your Honda CR-V. I took the liberty of swiping the key fob from your handbag while you were out jogging. Having ditched my own SUV, yours will be the perfect way to make my escape—before the cops piece it together—eventually making my way out of the country, where I'll never be found."

Giselle wrinkled her nose. "You're insane," she hissed at him unapologetically. "Killing someone who detests you won't change that!" *I can't believe I ever saw any redemptive qualities in him*, she told herself with major regrets.

Justin chuckled. "Believe me, I've been called worse," he snorted and ran the knife down her top without penetrating the skin just yet. "And I've been called more favorable names too—by you, Jenna…even Jacinta," he argued satisfyingly.

Giselle sneered and said sarcastically, while trying to buy time that she feared she didn't have much more of, "Maybe we all saw something in you, Justin, that's still there somewhere. It's not too late to stop this and give yourself up with no more killing or stealing money from your clients…"

"You do what you need to do to survive," he muttered as a lame excuse for perpetrating white-collar crimes in betraying those who trusted him the most. "My clients, pompous and sickening at times, got what they deserved." His mouth tightened. "So will you. But first, just out of curiosity, are you sleeping with the trooper you're staying with…?"

Giselle saw the pathological jealousy in his bloodshot eyes at the thought that she had actually found someone in Quincy, who was far more alluring, sensitive, strong and earning of her love and affections than Justin had even been or would be. She found herself answering him brazenly, even at risk of spurring on his resentment, "That's none of your business!"

"That's where you're wrong," Justin countered. "Everything about you is my business. If I can't have you, I sure as hell will make sure he can't either. Or anyone else! Say goodbye, Giselle…"

She braced herself for what was to come but was determined to keep Quincy in her thoughts to the very end of her life, if it came to that—not wanting Justin to win his desperate bid to even control her thinking in these waning moments. Or who she wished to have spent the rest of her life with.

QUINCY FEARED THAT he might have underestimated Justin Buckner's fixation on Giselle and the man's uncanny ability to carry out his acts of criminality almost with impunity—including managing to dodge the authorities and the hunt for the fugitive. That included Buckner being damned lucky enough to buy time when his ultimate capture was delayed by a case of mistaken identity.

Turned out that his lookalike, Larry Purnell, had fled from authorities because of an outstanding warrant for his arrest on drug trafficking and bootlegging charges. This had the effect of having the investigators take their eye off the real ball temporarily. Or long enough for Buckner to remain free and ever dangerous.

Now, after Miriam reported spotting the killer suspect's SUV just practically a stone's throw from Quincy's front door, it was apparent to him what he had already ascertained in Justin Buckner's warped mindset—that Buckner was going for broke in targeting Giselle to kill, having been able to successfully track her whereabouts.

I can't let that happen and won't, Quincy told himself, determined to prevent Buckner from taking away the life of the woman Quincy had fallen head over heels for. The fact that Giselle had not responded to his repeated attempts to reach her by phone was troubling, to say the least. He sped down the road in his SUV and through spotty traffic, barreling toward his house to divert disaster. Hot on his heels were members of law enforcement from various agencies, nearly as determined to put an end to Justin Buckner's thumbing his nose at anyone who took issue with his criminality.

As far as Quincy was concerned, he had much more to lose than anyone else, should Buckner succeed in adding another person to his list of homicide victims. The thought of Giselle dying before he had the opportunity to express how he felt about her was unimaginable to Quincy. This had to end today. But not in the way Buckner intended.

Quincy reached his property and exited the vehicle without ado before dashing toward the house to confront his nemesis. Inside, he spotted Muffin wandering across the floor, looking hapless and helpless but still alive.

Then Quincy heard voices coming from a room on the second floor—Giselle was being confrontational with Buckner, no doubt trying to buy time in pushing the unstable suspect's buttons—and drew his gun as he headed up the stairs.

"WAIT!" GISELLE SHOUTED, as Buckner seemed more than ready to plunge the knife into her. Likely the same weapon he'd used to stab Jacinta repeatedly, fully intending to kill. It made Giselle nauseous just thinking about it. Right now, though, her very survival hung in the balance. The pepper spray was still in her pocket, but she wasn't in the best position to remove it and use it before he could knife her. "Can't we talk about this?" she threw out desperately.

Justin peered at her and replied frostily, "I think

we've said all that needs to be said, Giselle, don't you?" He never allowed a response, when adding, "Say hello to Jenna for me, if you run into her on the other side."

As the level of his depravity sank in, Giselle heard the commanding voice of Quincy utter, "I wouldn't do that if I were you, Buckner. Drop the knife! Now!"

Giselle gazed at Quincy, who was inside the room and aiming his firearm at Justin. If she'd anticipated that he would simply give up, she was sorely mistaken, as she was quickly grabbed by Justin and placed between himself and Quincy.

Before she knew it, Justin had put the knife up to her throat. "I think it's the other way around, Trooper Lankard," he hissed. "You drop the weapon, or I'll just slice her throat right now and take Giselle's pretty head off while I'm at it—before you can even get off a clean shot. So, what's it going to be?"

"Don't do it, Quincy," Giselle pleaded, fearing that losing any leverage they had would be disastrous for both of them.

But Quincy saw it differently, clearly unwilling to sacrifice her life for his own as he lowered the gun while holding firmly onto it.

That gave Justin just enough time to surprise Giselle in using his free hand to remove a handgun from his jacket pocket. Without warning or time for Quincy to react, Justin shot him squarely in the chest.

Giselle screamed as Quincy went down, grimacing with discomfort. The gun slipped from his hand.

Justin told her testily, "Shut up! I want the ABI trooper to watch me slice your throat—" he tucked the firearm back inside his pocket while brandishing the knife "—and then I'm going to shoot him in the head so it's the last thing he ever sees…"

While Justin was preoccupied with his wicked and deadly plan of action, Giselle used the moment she'd been afforded to slip the pepper spray from her pocket. Before he knew what hit him, she sprayed it liberally into Justin's eyes and up his nose and inside his open mouth as he cried out with fury and yelled an expletive at her. He dropped the knife and rubbed his eyes vigorously.

Giselle seized another opportunity and smashed her fist into Justin's nose as hard as she possibly could— hearing the cracking of bones inside while he howled in even more pain like a wounded animal. She tried to reach for his gun, but he grabbed her wrist hard, threw her up against the wall and tried to strangle her, wrapping strong hands around her neck.

As she gasped for air, lungs burning, Giselle watched as Quincy somehow managed to get to his feet and pulled Justin away from her. Then he hit the killer with two solid blows to his shattered and bloody nose and added a stiff uppercut to his chin.

Justin went down like a sack of potatoes yet was able to maintain consciousness and dug inside his pocket for the gun, aiming it blindly in Quincy's direction.

A shot rang out.

It hit Justin in the forehead, and he went down instantly.

Giselle turned toward the entrance and saw ABI Trooper Alan Edmonston standing there, still pointing his Glock 22 service pistol at the downed fugitive. "Sorry I was a little late getting to the party," he spoke humorlessly.

"In this instance, much better late than never," Quincy quipped and then winced in pain.

Giselle put her arms on his shoulders worriedly. "Justin shot you…"

"Yeah, he did." Quincy unbuttoned his shirt and said, "Fortunately I was wearing a ballistic vest. The shot was enough to knock me off my feet and bruise some ribs, but I'll live."

"Thank goodness for that," she voiced cheerfully. "If anything had happened—"

"I know." He kept a straight face. "I wouldn't give him that satisfaction." Regarding her keenly, Quincy held Giselle's shoulders and asked measuredly, "Are you all right? Did he hurt you?"

"Aside from planning to stab me to death with that knife over there—" Giselle slanted her eyes to where the weapon had landed on the floor "—and attempting to strangle me, not really," she said sarcastically. She angled her eyes at the orange roses scattered across the floor. "He even handed me those roses as part of his dark sense of humor. He wanted me dead. Thanks to you and Alan, Justin never got to do what he'd fully intended."

"His loss," Quincy said mockingly, "and the orange roses are emblematic of that."

"True," she concurred. They both eyed Alan as he moved swiftly over to Justin and did a cursory examination. Giselle asked him, ill at ease, "Is he…?"

"Yeah," Alan responded equably. "The suspect has been put down and won't hurt you or others anymore."

She breathed a sigh of relief that her long nightmare had come to an end and told them, "Justin admitted to killing Neve, Yuki Sadie and attempting to murder Jacinta—as well as bilking his clients…and didn't seem to have any misgivings for his actions."

"Not surprising for a psychopath—and a greedy, selfish one at that," Quincy stated flatly. "But at least it stops here."

"Yes," she concurred and gazed at her dead ex-fiancé, feeling no sympathy.

"I'll call this in," Alan said and stepped out of the room, giving them a moment alone.

After he left, Quincy moved closer to Giselle, held her hands and locked eyes with her as he said, "With all that's happened, my timing may be off here, but you should know that I'm in love with you, Giselle."

Her eyes lit up in that instant, holding his gaze, and she responded in kind, "As far as I'm concerned, your timing is perfect, Quincy—since I'm very much in love with you too."

He smiled. "Is that so?"

"It's absolutely so," she promised.

"Well, in that case, guess I'm permitted to do this, without any hesitation as to how we feel about one another…"

Quincy took her cheeks and planted a sensual kiss on Giselle's mouth, which she was only too happy to reciprocate.

The spell was broken, though, when the house was suddenly swarming with law enforcement, crime scene technicians and personnel from the State Medical Examiner's Office as reality set in that a wanted fugitive had been brought down on the premises and the follow-up investigation began.

A MONTH LATER, Quincy sat at his desk going over the file on Justin Buckner now that the case had been closed insofar as the various crimes attributed to the man in Alaska over several harrowing weeks.

Stalking Giselle in and out of Taller's Creek and eventually trying to murder her was certainly first and foremost in Quincy's mind. The mere thought of Buckner having succeeded in his master plan at revenge made him want to puke, given the deep love Quincy had for Giselle.

As it was, the eight-inch serrated knife Buckner had wanted to stab her to death with was the same weapon used to attack Jacinta Cruz—with her DNA found on the blade—who was now all but fully recovered.

Then there was the gun Buckner had shot Quincy with as a prelude to the killer's plan to murder him. Being protected by ballistic body armor had saved his life but had been no less traumatic and had averted disaster for any future plans. The firearm itself was a Colt Cobra .38 Special revolver that, as it turned out, the Bureau of Alcohol, Tobacco, Firearms and Explosives National Tracing Center and National Integrated Ballistic Information Network had been able to link the illegal firearm to a murder in Fairbanks, Alaska, last year. The convicted killer, Aurelio McDermott, had apparently sold the murder weapon, which had eventually been purchased by Buckner on the black market in Anchorage.

Luckily he failed to make me another homicide victim, along with Giselle, Quincy told himself, feeling grateful to that effect as he stared at the laptop. Still, Buckner had, unfortunately, taken the lives of locals Neve Chenoweth, Yuki Kotake and Sadie Pisano, while Jacinta Cruz had barely survived her assault. Though the physical evidence was not as rock-solid for the murders as Quincy would have liked, there was enough of it, in addition to forensic and corroborating evidence, along with Buckner's confession to the crimes to both Giselle and Jacinta, to make Quincy comfortable with the belief that Buckner was guilty as sin on all counts.

Same was true for the Virginia murder of Jenna Sweeney, whose one mistake had been becoming the first object of Buckner's unnatural attention. The authorities in Chesapeake had essentially closed the books on the case, believing that there was enough forensic and circumstantial evidence to pin her death on Buckner.

Lastly, the feds' case against Justin Buckner as a crooked certified financial planner had also been put to rest in that the evidence overwhelmingly supported his guilt for embezzlement, wire fraud and related crimes. Attempts were still ongoing to try and recover some of the stolen funds for swindled clients.

Quincy sat back and turned his thoughts to Giselle. Things could not be going any better for them ever since they'd declared their love for one another. She was everything he could ever have hoped for in a woman and partner in a romantic relationship.

But now came the hard part. Was she truly ready to settle down into a life of marital happiness with him? He had deliberately delayed popping the question to give Giselle the needed time to get past the headache of Justin Buckner and decide if she wanted to remain in Alaska to become an ABI investigator's wife and mother of his future children.

Or if—now that Buckner was no longer an impediment—Giselle wanted to return to Chesapeake and the life she fled from, picking up where she left off as a dance instructor.

Though the thought of losing her scared Quincy as much as he was freely willing to admit, worse would be to keep Giselle in Alaska, while constantly second-guessing her decision at the expense of their happiness.

To that end, Quincy had come to a decision on whether or not he was willing to give up working for the Alaska Department of Public Safety's Division of Alaska State Troopers in order to be with the woman he loved.

It was an easy choice. Being with Giselle in Virginia or anywhere else was worth relocating and taking his career in law enforcement with him.

Now it was time that he put his money where his heart and soul already were etched in stone.

GISELLE JOGGED down the street near her apartment, after having just paid Jacinta a visit. Her recovery from the knife attack by Justin had been nothing short of miraculous. The documentary filmmaker was back at doing what she loved best—and ever grateful for the show of support amongst her friends and colleagues. Jacinta refused to allow Giselle to blame herself in any way for lowering her own guard in being attracted to Justin's alter ego, Jesse—knowing full well that Justin had been charming enough to lure most any woman into his web of deceit and murder, whether Giselle had been his own unhealthy fixation or not.

Accepting this truth for what it was, Giselle was happy to try and return to a normal life, as much as possible. Without the anvil of Justin to weigh her down, as had been the case for too long, now that he was dead and buried. That normality included getting back to running and enjoying the incredible landscape Alaska had to offer during her runs, along with friendly wildlife she encountered periodically.

Most of all, though, Giselle loved spending time with Quincy, the man of her dreams who had come to life in one magnificent and well-built package of masculinity and heroism. She had returned to living at her own place, so as not to make him feel pressure to move to the next level in their relationship—marriage and all it entailed, including starting a family. Yes, she wanted it all, but only when the time was right for both of them and not just on her own time schedule.

Whenever Quincy is ready to ask me to marry him, I'll be his for the taking, Giselle told herself, as she jogged home, where she was making dinner for Quincy tonight, while leaving the choice for dessert up to him.

Epilogue

When he arrived at Giselle's apartment that evening, Quincy was, by his own admission, a bit nervous about what he had planned. Though confident about the results, it didn't take away the butterflies in his stomach one bit.

He knocked on the door, still wearing his work clothes. While he had considered going over to his place to change, Quincy knew that Giselle thought he was *hot* in his uniform, so he stuck with it. But would gladly wear whatever suited her fancy when they were together in their private lives.

She opened the door and greeted him with a gorgeous smile and kiss, then said, "Right on time."

"I couldn't agree more," he replied, grinning, gazing at her in a nice floral sundress and clog sandals. Just then, Muffin came up to them and rubbed against his leg, telling Quincy that she almost certainly wanted him to pick her up, which he did. "Hey there, friend," he said with a laugh, cuddling the kitten.

"Guess you've got her totally hooked," Giselle said, chuckling. She added sweetly, "Just like someone else I know."

"Works both ways." Quincy colored, feeling the love as thick as molasses. "And with you, too, Muffin." He left no doubt.

Minutes later, they were having dinner, consisting of tuna-noodle casserole, lima beans and apple muffins with red wine.

After listening to Giselle talk about her day, Quincy spooned some lima beans and said coolly, "So, the ABI has closed the investigation on Justin Buckner."

She lifted a brow. "Really?"

"Yeah. We were able to tie enough of the pieces together to make the case for holding Buckner fully accountable for the crimes he perpetrated in this state." Quincy sipped wine. "If anything else comes up, we'll certainly be happy to look into it. But for now, the case has been wrapped up. That ghost won't be haunting you anymore."

Giselle ate some casserole and said with an exaggerated sigh, "Well, I'm really glad to hear that it's finally finished. Honestly, I'm so over Justin and all the bad things he did in this world."

"Good. Me too." Quincy took a breath and nibbled on a muffin, while eyeing her musingly. "There's something else I want to talk to you about," he put forth tentatively.

She held his gaze as she tasted wine tensely. "Okay…"

It's all come down to this moment—better not blow it, Quincy told himself, steeling his nerves as he dabbed his mouth with a paper napkin. He waited a beat, then said straightforwardly, "You know how I feel about you, Giselle, and I'm pretty sure I know how you feel about me. So, now that the dust has been settled and swept away,

I don't want to wait any longer to take the next crucial step in our lives…"

He got off his chair and dropped to one knee, where he removed a yellow-diamond engagement ring with an eighteen-karat yellow-gold band from his shirt pocket, took her hand and slipped the ring onto her finger for a perfect fit. "I'm madly in love with you, Giselle Kinard, and I'm asking you to become my wife and a person I can build a terrific future with—including the most wonderful children we can bring into this world—sharing our cultures and life's lessons. Whether you want to live in Alaska, Virginia or elsewhere, I'll happily go where you go. If you say yes, you'll make me the happiest state trooper in Alaska, if not the entire country!"

Giselle's eyes watered as she said without hesitation, "Yes, I will definitely marry you, Quincy Lankard, and gladly become your wife and mother of any children we are so very blessed to have together."

"Seriously?" He flashed his teeth and wanted to make certain he heard her correctly.

"Yes, yes and yes again—a million times yes!" Giselle voiced delightedly. She looked at her engagement ring, marveling at it. "And just for the record, Trooper Lankard, I'm quite happy making our home in Alaska, thank you, and will be even happier to do so as Mrs. Lankard. I love the idea of integrating our cultures, upbringing and views on life into our children's lives as we cultivate their futures."

"Wonderful!" Getting to his feet, Quincy was all smiles as he pulled Giselle up and into his arms. "Thank you for being you and finding your way into my life."

"Back at you," she gushed, angling her mouth to wait for his lips to meet hers.

He didn't disappoint as Quincy kissed her passionately, knowing that what they had could not be duplicated and he wouldn't want to. Giselle was everything he wanted and needed in a soulmate, and he would make sure the same was true in reverse.

When they later spilled the beans with his parents and sister, they were over the moon with enthusiasm about adding an important new member to the family in Giselle, who was clearly just as eager to become part of his family as Quincy had known she would be, in giving her a sense of belonging that had been missing in her life.

A YEAR LATER, Giselle Lankard was at Taller's Creek Dance Studio on Windeer Drive, with her popular class for ballroom dancing in full swing. Six months ago, she had seen a dream come true in opening up the eight-thousand-square-foot facility in Southcentral Alaska, which had become her permanent home, with occasional visits to Chesapeake, Virginia, and elsewhere with her husband, Quincy.

Now she was truly living the dream and able to bring what she knew and loved to the local community—offering dance classes for the young, old and everyone in between. Including a variety of dance instruction and programs for beginners, experienced dancers, dance competitions, summer camps and even private lessons.

Wearing a maroon tank leotard, gray leg warmers and black character dance shoes, Giselle had her long black hair—happy to have it back to its natural color—in a topknot bun as she moved graciously between the dance couples, giving instructions along the way.

"Wonderful," she spoke cheerfully to an attractive, white-haired older couple who were celebrating their forty-fifth anniversary by learning how to ballroom dance. Then Giselle told a younger, well-groomed handsome couple that looked like they belonged on the covers of magazines, "You're nailing it!"

All the pairs—and even a few singles—seemed just as eager to master the steps and dance fluidly to the beat of Latin American music.

It was only when she saw the handsome gentleman enter the studio that Giselle's heart did a little leap and check. A big smile spread across her face as she broke away from the dancers and met him halfway.

"Hey," Quincy said, flashing his own toothy grin while dressed in casual attire and comfortable shoes.

"You made it." Giselle tilted her face upward and gave him a kiss on the lips.

"Of course. Just had to ditch the work clothes and get over here."

"Good." She smiled, grateful to have the love of her life on her turf. "Ready to do some ballroom dancing?"

"Yeah, definitely." He glanced about at the couples on the floor. "Looks like you have your hands full today."

"What can I say? Everyone loves to dance," she quipped.

"Hmm…" Quincy gave her the benefit of a level and curious gaze. "Any chance a guy could get a private lesson here?"

Giselle beamed. "Thought you'd never ask." She tiptoed and whispered into his ear, "It'll be cleared out in fifteen minutes. Then I'm all yours."

He grinned sideways, taking her hands. "Wouldn't have it any other way."

"And most definitely, neither would I," she assured him gleefully.

* * * * *

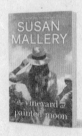